GW00692083

UNTHOLOGY 5
2014

To Catherine
Elizabeth Ines. 28-/06/14

UNTHANK BOOKS

First published in 2014
By Unthank Books
www.unthankbooks.com

Printed in England by Imprint, UK

All Rights Reserved

A CIP record for this book is available from the
British Library

Any resemblance to persons fictional or real who are living,
dead or undead is purely coincidental.

ISBN 978-1-910061-00-8

Edited by Ashley Stokes and Robin Jones

Cover by Tommy Collin

A Little More Prayer © Angela Readman 2014; *Daddy's Little Secret* © KS Silkwood 2014; *Red* © Roelof Bakker 2014; *A Writer Tries to Work It Out* © Jose Vargese 2014; *The Regular* © Mark Mayes 2014; *Restoration* © Sarah Bower 2014; *79 Green Gables* © John D Rutter 2014; *Death and the Maiden* © Maggie Ling 2014; *The Lesser God* © Andrew Oldham 2014; *The Coroner's Report* © Victoria Heath 2014; *Kowalski* © Garrie Fetcher 2014; *Carrie and You* © Elizabeth Baines 2014; *Fresh Water* © Charles Wilkinson 2014; *The End of the World* © CS Mee 2014.

CONTENTS

UNTHOLOGY 5

Introduction
The Editors

Can I Write?

Can I write about a little pig that lives in a bidet? Can I write about a space alien on trial for being a Muslim? Can I write to confess my possession of a shaming micropenis? Can I write to become the messiah of the similarly afflicted? Can I write about spoons, swoons and squamous baboons? Can I write about how Heidegger invented Tedium-Worship? Can I write about his indifference to the torture and murder of millions? Can I write a reformulation of Camus' question about what good it does to 'theoretically liberate the individual' if we 'allow a man to be subjugated under certain conditions'? Can I write about spanners? Can I write about planks? Can I write about prawns? Can I write about cryptids? Can I write about hoaxes and versions? Can I write about YouScratchMyBackYouScratchMyBackism? Can I write about SoggyBiscuitImperialism? Can I write *Morbida the Condescending Vampire*? Can I write *The Cloning of Spassky*? Can I write *They Saved Spassky's Brain*? Can I write about the agents of B.A.L.D? Can I write *The Yellow Swastika*? Can I write *Mimsy and Mumford*? Can I write

Splash and Weasel? Can I write *The Struggle for The Trestle*? Can I write *The Man With Two Left Brains*? Can I write *Depression Logic: If the Game is Rigged, Don't Play*? Can I write of my **Terrible Dread** at certain events? Can I write of our joy at *Project U*? Can I write of our great appreciation of your support and encouragement? Can I write of our regard for your company? Can I write to announce that *Unthology* is now a twice-yearly campaign? Can I write of Angela Readman? Can I write of KS Silkwood? Can I write of Roelof Baker? Can I write of Jose Vargese? Can I write of Mark Mayes? Can I write of Sarah Bower? Can I write of John D Rutter? Can I write of Maggie Ling? Can I write of Andrew Oldham? Can I write of Victoria Heath? Can I write of Garrie Fletcher? Can I write of Elizabeth Baines? Can I write of Charles Wilkinson? Can I write of CS Mee?

Unthology 5, alive and thriving.
Forza Unthank!

The Editors

A Little More Prayer

Angela Readman

Some things exist in one place, one time, and with only one person. It's like speaking a language no one understands because they didn't live the only moments that can teach it. I couldn't tell them everything.

I sipped hot chocolate and stared at the photo. Nodded, yes, that's him. He was younger. The photo looked like it had snapped part of him away.

'We know this is difficult,' they said.

I felt their gaze flit over my head and land on my face; a box of tissues was pushed across the desk. I touched his paper face. The photograph looked like he'd just been raking the lawn, smiling, the day the picture was taken, that he'd do these things always. It was hard to believe it was the same guy, maybe only fifteen years older, but less in the eyes. Where did it go?

'Don't worry. We'll find him,' they said.

I watched them talk through the glass wall, Mom's mouth opened and closed. They were done asking questions, for now. Walking out, Mom opened the door, allowing me to go first. I looked at her pale hand on the handle. This is what a kid glove must look like, I thought.

'They'll catch that shit,' she said, driving away.

Some people called him a monster, a sicko, a pervert, not Mom. She used to work as a chambermaid; shit was the worst. I stared out the car window at the store that sold cheap toilet seats. Everything she wanted to ask wedged in the car between the driver and the passenger seat. I looked outside, let her have her shit rather than explain.

*

My eyes opened.

'Are you OK?' were his first words.

He had a long face, weathered like a garbage man. I looked around. Where was I? I'd been walking through the cemetery on my way home. No rush. The sun made cool shadows of the gravestones; I bent to inspect something on the ground. Shiny. Red. I looked closer; it was a plastic rose. I smelt cut grass, then something like the dentists. Kick. Bite. Scream. Kick. One big hand clamped a cloth over my mouth. Then I was gone.

It was cool and dim wherever I was now. There was a wooden beamed ceiling overhead. I looked at my hands like the hands of a girl saying her prayers, bound at the wrists with the same blue nylon rope the neighbours hung their washing on. My ankles were tied.

'You OK?' he said again, slipping the bandana out of my mouth.

The sound burst out, higher than I thought I could be. He stuffed the fabric back in.

Don't think I didn't fight, I told them. Even in my sleep, I kicked, he said. I fought to wake up, escape where I was, who I was and who he was - a sixteen-year-old girl and a grown man, and what the combination must mean. He lowered the gag. I spat. He dropped the water bottle in his hand.

'We'll try again,' he said, 'no one can hear you, but you gotta be quiet to eat.'

He held the water to my lips. I swallowed. He unwrapped a sandwich from its plastic triangular house and I ate from his hand.

'That better?' he said.

It was. That sandwich was bacon and lettuce. I don't know why I remember, I just do. I looked at the dust on the floorboards swept into arcs like he'd cleaned. Trays of green rat poison squatted under the eaves. I sat, mattress beneath me and a My Little Pony duvet over my knees.

'What you going to do to me? You sick fucking...'

He never learnt what sick fucking thing he was. The bandana stuffed the words back into my mouth. I sobbed. Lifting my tied arms, I swung out, cracking my knuckles on the low beams. He pushed me back. Held me tight.

'Don't move. You're going to hurt yourself,' he said.

He was shaking, fist raised, mid-air. I watched his fist turn back into hand.

'Don't make me do this, please,' he said.

I looked down. I couldn't see my hands. Both were clasped in his to stop me banging them on the eaves.

Rain drip dropped on the roof. I woke with a furry rabbit stuffed between my arms. He was there, hunched over me, the slight curve at the top of his back pressed against the tiles, the apology of a boy who got tall too fast. The rain died. He turned his back, took off his wet shirt and replaced it with another from a bag.

There were cracks in the tiles, chinks of sky. He stuffed plastic bags into the gaps.

'I didn't want you to get rained on,' he said.

I opened my mouth. Nothing came. No one got wet to keep me dry before, I thought. It may not make him a good guy, but it occurred to me I might not die. Maybe he just wanted something to shelter from the rain.

Something cold rattled. I shook off the duvet. The chain was looped around one ankle with a padlock. The other end was padlocked to a truss in the roof. Now my legs weren't tied together, I stood. One. Two. Three. Four. Five paces from the mattress. There was soda, a muffin and a bucket and tissues within reach. He was gone. I strained towards a hatch in the floor. Too far. I stomped the floor, rattled, stomped, rattled and stomped. I pushed at the tiles above me. Solid.

I sat down, out of breath. I thought about the yellow-headed blackbird that once flew into the kitchen flapping, wings battering against the walls to find a window. I'd stood with a pan in my hand and the keys to the back door. I could do nothing until it calmed down. They'd be looking for me. Any second now they'd find me. Any minute, any day. Any week.

*

Birds hopped across the roof, Tap. Tappety Tap Tap. I listened to a lawn mower outside. Sunlight sliced through the gaps in the tiles and striped my hands. What day was it? I was learning each day made different sounds. It must be a weekday when I heard diggers. And it must be Monday, if I heard digging the day after I heard bells. I knew I was in the church. When was it open? I recalled the locked door and beer bottles on the steps.

Most mornings, he left me alone. I supposed he worked. I'd be in math about now, I thought. I imagined Carrie Strutt rolling her eyes at Mr Stock's damp armpits. I thought of the test I was missing, the gossip, the hanging around. The sun moved, slotting between tiles on the other side of the roof. Around this time last week, I was walking home. Mom was already at work. She wouldn't know I was missing till after her shift. Even then, I wasn't sure she'd know.

'Just like her to pull this shit to drive you crazy,' Bill would say. 'She's probably got a fake ID somewhere.'

I pictured Mom shaking her head, heeding to the word of her all knowing latest guy. Later, she might go through my room, look for missing clothes, the diary I gave up on when I was ten. I lied to it anyway, only wrote stuff that would make me look good if it fell into the wrong hands.

I never told Mom what I thought about while I was gone. I closed my eyes and remembered the exact smell of the kitchen – fried things and something like lettuce going limp. I recalled the sticky feeling of peeling the loose plastic strip off the edge of the coffee table in the den, and even the sound of Bill's cough in the morning waking me up like a cock crowing in the dawn. When I was missing, I thought I'd tell them everything if I got the chance, but the words faded in front of their faces. Home was more vivid when I wasn't there.

Footsteps on the stairs. Someone was coming. They'd barge in with guns. The hatch opened with a whine. He put down a brown bag.

'You hungry?' he said, lowering the gag.

He was breathless as someone winning a race. He emptied the bag and lined up the contents like prizes on a game show. Sandwiches, soda, peanut butter cups, toothpaste, a pearly purple toothbrush, a pack of cards and a magazine. I reached for the magazine with both hands. (I don't know why; I just wanted something that felt normal, I think.) A kid pressed her cheek against the nose of a horse on the cover. It looked like something eight year olds who dream of flying ponies read.

'Do you like it?' he said.

'It's too young for me.'

His cheeks reddened. The words slapped.

'I like purple,' I said, looking at the toothbrush.

'Which you like better, tuna or cheese?' he said, waving sandwiches.

'I like 'em both,' I said, 'really.'

I felt bad about the magazine. He didn't have to bring it. He didn't have to give me anything. It reminded me of the paper cocktail umbrella's Mom used to bring me back from the bar. Every night she brought me a little something, like part of me was with her at work, tugging her hand and pointing out shiny things. Then, she didn't bring me a thing. I was too old. She was too busy laughing at customer's jokes.

He peeled apart the sandwiches. One slice of each was loaded with filling; the other was mostly mayo. He pressed the cheese-laden bread to the tuna loaded slice and handed me the sandwich. Quietly, we ate. He sat watching.

'What's your favourite card game?' he said.

'I don't know any.'

I spoke softly, listening for someone, anyone, who might hear.

'I'll teach you,' he said.

I could hear no one. He dealt cards I held with tied hands. I'd play. Wait.

I never told anyone about the games. They didn't ask. Somehow it seemed trivial; it didn't match the way they spoke to me, careful, as if the wrong tone would topple me like a house of cards. But we did play games, every night. Twenty questions, Poker, Jenga and Connect Four. I considered the clatter and saw he wasn't afraid of being overheard. I struggled with pieces in my tied hands and he undid the rope. I lifted the Connect Four board and swung. He retied the rope and picked scattered yellow and red pieces off the floor.

'I'm disappointed in you,' he said.

I was disappointed myself.

'You promise to play nice this time?'

I did. Later, they'd say I was smart, to gain his trust and not fight. I didn't tell them the urge just wasn't always there. Everyday I waited. And when they didn't come, I wondered what it would be like if no one came. What if even he never came back? Ever. Who'd bring soda and say goodnight? I smiled when the hatch lifted. It's OK. *He's back. I won't starve to death.* He grinned. One tiny smile, a twitch of relief, was everything to him. He looked like I'd run to him with open arms.

I saw the photo on his sleeping bag he rolled out over the hatch. It was a girl.

'That your daughter?' I said.

He snatched it up as if looking would steal part of her face.

'What's her name?'

'Jessica.'

'What happened to her?'

'Gone.'

The photo curled in the tightening cradle of his palm. The girl, of maybe six, wore bunches, a blue skirt and a T-shirt of a unicorn. The photo was faded as if it once lived by a sunlit window. I pictured the kids in my street in bright hot pants and cut-off tops. The photo looked old. I glanced at the magazine with horses on the cover and tips on how to look after your kitten inside.

'You know,' I said, 'she'd be older now. She probably wouldn't care about ponies anymore.'

He leaned close, head tilted as a dog listening for its owner to come home.

'Tell me what she'd care about now,' he said.

So I told him stuff, stuff his daughter, I imagined was dead, would have liked and grown out of. I flicked through the catalogue of dreams in girls heads, remembering shit I forgot I used to care about. I'd wanted a pony too, I said, then I realised I couldn't ride. Once, I saw a man fall off a horse on TV and my hand went to my nose instantly, protecting myself from the damage dreaming of ponies might do to me.

'Then what did you want?' he said.

The last time someone asked me what I wanted, I think I was so sick I couldn't keep anything down.

I told him about dancing, pictures on my wall of young women with arms like the pale necks of swans.

'I walked tip toe everywhere for a year,' I said.

And I told him, at twelve, I learnt I was too old to be a great ballerina, to start now. It was too late. Next, I thought I'd be model, but I wasn't tall. I saw a show with a shit load of waiting around and couldn't stand the idea of spending my life just waiting for the perfect photo to come out. I just wanted someone to open a magazine and be jealous of a smile that came out right the first time round.

'Now what?' he said, 'what do you dream about now?'

What would his daughter's dreams have been diluted to by now? Boys, I guessed. None in particular, none I wanted so much as the buzz of stealing one off the most popular girls in school. I didn't tell him this. He was listening so hard. I had the world in my mouth; I couldn't bring it crashing down. I ran out of words. Other than going home, I didn't know what I wanted now. Back home, my only dream was to leave.

'My grades aren't great. Those sorts of girls seem to do make-up or hair or something,' I said, 'I'll wind up doing that, I guess.'

If he released me I'd study more. I'd be better at loads of shit: learn martial arts, how to pick a lock, study psychology; tell my mother I loved her, maybe. I made mental promises to no one in particular. Not all could be kept.

'Let me go,' I said.

He turned his back, rather than see me cry.

Something changed after that conversation. He asked what I'd like from the store. I read the same magazines I wanted at home, ate the same burritos, got extra cheese. Most things I asked for he brought me, except a pen or pencil. They were weapons, he said. Crayons were fine. The biggest change was my hands weren't tied. They were free to draw with wax crayons like a kid who paints rainbows to blot out rainy days. I closed my eyes, then drew a fading lemon house with scabs of grass out front, a red kettle, and what I recalled of the view from my bedroom, the big underwear of the neighbour on the line.

'Spit out your gum,' he said.

He ripped the gum and stuck my pictures of home to the beams. I wondered when Mom stopped putting my work on the fridge, when I became too old to be proud. The house got erased of all evidence of me when Bill moved in, except for my room.

'That's a real pretty picture.'

He smiled, staring at my paper wavering on a draft in the roof. I felt bad. The real reason I asked for the crayons was to rat him out.

I reached up and pushed bits of paper through a crack in the tiles, my tiny letterbox to the world.
I am Cory Hastings. I think I'm in a church.

The cracks weren't big enough for letters that weren't thin. The crayons weren't fine enough to write small. Each SOS was brief. They started as me, then became third person. Don't ask why.

The missing girl is alive & locked in a church.

Cory Hastings is in the roof.

I imagined the wind sweeping my words up off the roof. I pictured a police officer picking up a note that landed at his feet like a lottery ticket on the street. The note with my name, where I was, and the date I went missing was too fat to fit. I folded it, pushing against the gap. Footsteps. The creak of hatch. I screwed up the paper, and dropped it to the floor. The sketchpad lay open to a drawing of a tree with a bird in it, a river of cassette tape flowed from its branches. I sat.

'I got you this,' he said.

He pulled a postcard with a photo of a kingfisher on from the bag.

'Thought you might like it,' he said. 'I see you sometimes, just listening to the birds.'

I touched the sunlight photographed to the bird's chest, its shiny beak.

'You did good,' I said.

He looked away. I think 'You did good' was close enough to 'I love you' for him. It's good enough for a lot of people, I think. I pictured Mom putting beer in the fridge as Bill watched

TV, and decided I'd never let it be enough for me.

He wandered around the attic picking up candy wrappers, the ball of paper in his hand. Shit. Don't open it. Please. I'm sorry. He scrunched the note tight and stuffed it into an empty plastic triangle our sandwiches came in.

I've searched for that postcard and never found the exact king-fisher. Not exactly the same. No one needs to know. They were more interested in the church and those last months when I followed him downstairs. It was strange to them. Dangerous. It felt natural at the time. First, I was gagged, then I wasn't, then he freed my hands. Now, he trusted me enough to let me go for a walk.

'Don't get any ideas,' he said, opening the hatch.

I followed. I couldn't get far without him grabbing me.

The prayer box was between me and him. We walked in the church amongst the waxy pews and stopped at the prayer box. He asked me to read the notes to him.

'What are people needing?' he said.

Mrs Jones prays for her husband to get better... Edith Piccard prays she'll find love. The prayers weren't so different-someone to get better, somewhere to live, something not to die.

I stopped reading. There was a slip of paper with my name on. Someone called Casey wanted me to be alive and well.

'Someone I don't know's praying for me,' I said.

'Everyone is,' he said.

'Everyone? What they saying?'

My heart raced like I was listening to gossip on the phone. I wanted to see the soap opera of my life.

'Missing girl, bright, lots of friends, honour roll stuff,' he said.

I smiled, never on the honour roll my whole life. I changed my friends as often as they changed their bras.

'Have I been on TV?'

'Sure. Posters too.'

'I want to see it,' I said. 'I wanna see what they say on the news. Can I?'

There was something about that 'can I?' he couldn't refuse. It was 'a can I?' that made him a father again and made me a little girl.

'Don't think I can get a TV to work in the attic,' he said. 'I can tape channel ten.'

And he did. Each night we walked through the vacant church to the TV in the preacher's study behind the altar. I sniffed the wicks of melted candles wondering how many were lit in my name.

I sat on the floor in front of the small TV and watched them talk about the missing girl - vibrant, popular, missed by her family and friends. I couldn't tear my eyes off screen. It's as close to going to their own funeral as anyone gets. It was like having more than one life.

Mom looked into the camera, right at me. 'Whoever has done this, we forgive you. We just want our daughter home,' she said, slowly.

I stared at the nylon jacket she wore for job interviews and funerals and wondered where her spine came from. Mom, who never got straight to the point her whole life, who got mad or sad and started talking thick and fast, now saying exactly what she needed to say. No more, no less.

'Bring our girl back safe,' she said.

She didn't fall to bits the way she did when Bill sometimes left. I thought crying and yelling was all she had. I went missing and something no one knew she possessed was born. I re-wound the tape to play it again. '*Our* daughter'... Who was the *our*? When did Bill include me? When did Dad start answering her calls? Why now?

'You want to see it again?'

'No,' I said.

We walked back through the church. He followed with the torch. 'You wanna go back upstairs?'

'Not yet,' I said. I emptied the prayer box, raking for my name. 'I want a little more prayers first.'

'That's what we all need,' he said, 'a little more prayers.'

I climbed through the hatch, forgetting to slip the crayoned note in my pocket into the box.

It was madness, they said, the risk of being caught he took by letting me walk in the church at night, because that's how it did end, with two maintenance guys seeing the torchlight and rushing in to catch what they assumed was a thief. Timber swung from their hands. He ducked, ran. I cried out, no words, just a cry.

*

I sipped the hot chocolate the female officer kept in her desk drawer. Phones rang, doors in corridors slammed, I winced. So loud. No, I said, he never mentioned any friends, didn't even talk about the girl in the photo, whom they said wasn't dead, but grown, taken overseas by her mother at five. No, he never spoke about any special place; I'd no idea where he went. No, no, he never touched me, not like that.

There's a hush in the house now, after Mom hugged me, let me go and stopped making pancakes. She watches me make a tuna sandwich and a cheese one, cut them into triangles and peel them apart. Bill finishes the milk. She asks what happened to that kid I saw a movie with.

'I didn't like the way he held my hand,' I say.

I wanted him to clasp both, hold them so tight they couldn't move. I flick a Jack of Diamonds in the air and Mom shrugs. She doesn't ask where I learnt to shuffle cards like a pro, when I started to sketch, or why there are so many postcards of kingfishers in my room. She looks at me sometimes, then looks away. I'm not sure I could explain. I'm not sure she wants to know.

Daddy's Little Secret

KS Silkwood

My name is George Ashford and late this afternoon I disposed of my daughter's body. My wife, Marie, does not yet know what I have done and is not yet concerned. No, I'll have to wait until this evening for her particular brand of amateur dramatics. By then it's likely that her lover will have already been informed. He will know because at this very moment they are together, and he will be the very first person Marie will phone when our daughter hasn't returned from school.

This morning I arranged with our daughter a little secret that she was not to tell anyone about. She was to meet me at the end of the road as soon as the bell went for home time. She would have to be quick because Daddy's a very busy man and she really couldn't afford to miss out on something as special as this.

Because Marie was with her lover she will hope that Sue, cheerful, dependable Sue, will have collected our daughter. Sue is ill today and Martin, her husband, collected their children in a rush between shifts. Martin works very hard for his family. He and Sue both work very hard for what they have. They have four children. Two boys and two girls. Marie and I have one child, our daughter, who we love very much.

I have lost the car. It's dark now and I've been walking for quite a while, which makes me realise how late it is. I feel in my suit jacket pocket and shake a set of keys: front door, back door, garage and car. Leaves clutter the drain, so I clear them a bit and at arm's length I drop the bundle into the gutter. A man and his young son walk briskly by, laughing together. For a moment I wish it was at me but it isn't. They don't notice me, don't see a smile that barely suppresses my envy, and don't notice what I finally now have.

Our front door is a deep red colour; which was not my choice. I would have chosen a yellow or an ochre. Marie decided on this colour. One day, I got back from work to discover that all the outside doors had been repainted on a whim. Marie's spontaneity was one of the characteristics that shone out when I first saw her.

A party, a surprise party for a work colleague. She was the caterer's assistant. I remember there was quite a fuss between the others. Who would like to do what and who would give it a go? They did try, but as they did, I knew, I had this feeling that she was cleverer than that. She had one of those looks that told you she wasn't impressed with boys and their bravado. We spoke briefly but politely over the salmon and avocado sauce, and after an hour we left the party. She just walked out without permission, and I followed, enjoying the envious glances from my colleagues. I can't really remember the exact details of what happened next but Marie is so impulsive, so in touch with herself and her sexuality. The doors used to be light blue with a white trim. I thought we had decided to paint them yellow or an ochre, something bright but easy on the eye, something more

The door opens and I'm slightly fazed by the hall light. As my eyes adjust I can see a large suitcase and a smaller checked one that we use for our daughter when we go on holiday. Marie is standing, just standing in the doorway. I'd like to get into my house but I'd have to push Marie out of the way. That thought crosses my mind but Marie turns and walks anxiously into the front room, talking in sounds that I can hardly hear. I pass the suitcases on my way to the kitchen. An ashtray falls onto the tiled floor as I lay my briefcase on the work surface. Marie has burst into the kitchen with furious eyes, spitting noise, but I can't make out what the noise is. It isn't a word or words, or a language that I can recognise or understand or ever understood; so I put the kettle on and lean against the sink. It's quiet now. I'm waiting for Marie to tell me what the problem is. She is looking at the floor, eyes scrunched up and breathing loudly through her nose.

Our daughter is missing. Marie tells me that she hasn't come home yet. I say that I thought she always picked up our daughter from school. Marie pauses. Sue should have but she is ill so Martin picked up the children. I say I'm not really all that clued up on the pick-up arrangements and ask why Sue was picking up our daughter?

Marie begins to rub her nose and nervously picks up the ashtray. Sighing, she tells me that today was a Sue day and that she was going to go round and collect our daughter after doing the shopping. If it was a Sue day, I start, then what happened when she went to the school? Marie curses under her breath and reminds me that Martin did it but that our daughter had gone by the time he had arrived. The kettle is whistling and as I reach for the tea bag jar my arm passes straight through the steam and I scald my wrist. It takes a second or two for me to react but Marie is already holding my hand and watching the bright red blotch appearing. She is still holding my hand as she runs cold water over it.

I look at her, all concerned and busy telling me off. I can't remember the last time she held my hand, held me with any concern or affection. I feel like crying. I feel fragile and I can't allow her to continue touching me. I pull my hand away at the exact moment she lets go to get some antiseptic cream.

I lick my wrist and I am in control again. I ask if the police have been notified. Marie shouts through from the conservatory confirming this and that she had to wait for me to get back from work. She'd tried to reach me there but couldn't get through and the police told her to wait in case I'd picked her up. Suddenly it's quiet, I can see Marie out of the corner of my eye but I keep looking at my wrist. She is looking at me. I glance at her quickly, and then again, but this time lingering.

My mind races as Marie asks why I am late. I smile and tell her I stopped off to buy some cakes for us to have after dinner. I left my wallet in the car and when I got back to the car it had gone and I had to walk home. She says to me that I've taken my time telling her this. I say to her, after nearly laughing out loud, that we've been a bit preoccupied.

Our daughter is missing. And the car being stolen is not important. It just doesn't matter.

I shouted this so loudly that Marie flinched and held herself, tightly squeezing her arms. I take the cream from her and let out a deep breath. I tell her I'm sorry and her eyes start to wet and her lip begins to tremble uncontrollably, gradually stretching over her teeth in a bizarre contortion. A mewing sob breaks out and she stands, arms still clenched tightly looking at me. I can see her face start to redden and blotch as it always does when she's upset. The usual bluey-green of her irises begin to bleach and dilute as the tears wash away the strain of our life together. I glare at her to show her I am still strong, that I at the very least can cope, but all the posturing dissolves the longer I see the hurt I am causing, the longer I watch her struggle to subdue the pain by chewing her lip.

The world has stopped for both of us and, as my own eyes begin to moisten, I pinch the bridge of my nose and turn away. I see the suitcases in the hall and I know that what was going to be an important day for Marie and our daughter has become a day when the inconceivable has happened: a change in the everyday routine of our life. Marie touches my arm, acknowledging that the suitcases represented a redirection in our marriage. She whispers to me two words, then repeats them, and I understand, I really understand. Strangely Marie looks beautiful, her eyes soft and needing. Our daughter is not coming home tonight, but in her absence it seems that something that had been missing has returned. Perhaps my beautiful wife was not with a lover. Perhaps she was busy preparing for a great task, one that was brave and inevitable.

I know I have not always been the best husband, and that I have pushed and have been pushed away, but this moment, this exact moment has clarified things for me. Whatever may be around the corner for us as a family, I am now aware of the one thing I think I had forgotten.

I look at Marie in those deep angelic eyes and pull her close towards me. She doesn't resist, doesn't pull away, and I start to cry. I hold her close, and, barely audible, I tell her I love her.

*

Marie and I are in bed. For the first time in months we made love. Through Marie's tears I could hear her expel the long deep breath of her orgasm. We made love like this once before after the stillbirth of our first child, Oliver. The disappointment I felt after Marie returned from hospital now seems to be equalled by the passivity of my performance. In one respect I have my Marie back. We are united again and this means we can be happy again; all the distractions that have been in the way for the past few years have been eradicated. But there is still something that is not quite right.

I can't sleep.

I lie on my back with my arms folded staring at the blue-lit ceiling. I like the curtains completely drawn and to be engulfed totally in the darkness of the night. Marie prefers the light of the moon to illuminate the bedroom. If it is light I can't sleep. If there is the slightest noise, I can hear it and can't sleep. I spent two weeks trying to work out where a low buzzing sound was coming from. Every night I'd listen while Marie fell straight to sleep unaware of my nocturnal pressures. If I lay with my head on the pillow it seemed louder but if I moved to the centre of my side of the bed it was quieter. I listened at the walls to see if next door had a machine or something against the wall that was vibrating and therefore keeping me awake. I'd think to myself that it wasn't always like this and as I got up and put my clothes on to go downstairs to make a cup of tea I'd be completely flummoxed and at times despairing. One night after considering that it might be the lamppost outside, I decided to turn the bedside light on. As I clicked the trigger I noticed an alarm clock.

I say an alarm clock because it wasn't my alarm clock. I never need one. I use my watch. I looked at the digital numbers telling me that it was four forty eight a.m. I had been awake in bed for over five hours. I listened carefully, very carefully to the low buzz it was making. I put my ear to the bedside cabinet and could hear the buzz vibrating through the wood. Smiling to myself, I turned to Marie and vaguely remembered her telling me that she'd bought the clock so that she didn't have to rely on me waking her as I left for work. In truth it was a sensible choice, because a wind up alarm clock would have kept both her and me awake because of the rhythm of the ticks. Not only that but perversely the red digital numbers would, she said, shock her if she woke during the night. And so that was why I had it on my side of the bed. As I looked at her sleeping head, I silently thanked her for her thoughtlessness.

Tonight we are sleeping with the alarm clock on top of three novels, which seems to insulate the vibration, and the curtain half drawn, letting the moonlight and the lamp post light project the silhouette of the window frame onto the bed and over me. Not Marie, the light doesn't reach that far across the bed, she's next to the bedroom door, which is normally ajar so that our daughter can easily slip in if she has had a nightmare or needs anything.

I can't sleep so I get up. It's chilly downstairs and the kitchen has a lino floor, which is cold for my bare feet. I look at the mug I had prepared earlier, still with the tea bag in it and the milk. There is a brown circle around the tea bag but it doesn't put me off. Usually I like to pour the water in straight after I've prepared the cup of tea so that I can strain the tea bag straight away to be sure that I have a hot cup of tea. Marie likes to let it brew, and consequently I end up with a vaguely warm mug of tea that has to be drunk immediately. I like my tea hot.

The night is starting to break into day and, finally, I am feeling tired. The tea has left my mouth feeling tinny and bitter. I look at the hallway clock and step quietly upstairs back to bed. I can still get a few hours before I have to get up for work. When I get into bed I am freezing, and to make matters worse Marie is very warm. She turns to me and smiles sleepily, putting her arm around me, and gradually I drift off to sleep.

*

Marie is already up when I awake. I can hear her in the kitchen where she is making breakfast. The only noise is the familiar clink and clank of crockery and knives and forks, expensive ones from a popular high street retailer. I don't particularly like them. The angle of the fork head is awkward, it's too flat and I struggle to employ it properly, leaving me numb, like I have no feeling in my left hand. I sit on the edge of the bed and look out of the window, Marie having opened the curtains, knowing that the morning light will rouse me. It is raining outside and the sky is grey and quiet. I ruffle what's left of my hair and get dressed for work. I don't want to shower today, it doesn't feel right. I pull the curtains closed and put my underwear on, then my socks and then my suit and tie. In this light I can barely see myself in the mirror. I blend in perfectly with the bedroom, dark and invisible against the sparsely decorated walls. There's a call. Breakfast is ready.

I don't really like to eat so much breakfast at 07:30 in the morning but I have a tendency to miss meals during the day due to the nature of my work, due to the fact I'm so busy all the time. I reach the bottom of the stairs where a large mirror hangs. It's another day, I tell myself, just another day. I turn towards the kitchen. I can see Marie at the sink, her back to me, doing something up. It is a flask. I don't need a flask for work. I don't need a flask because we have vending machines. Marie turns as I reach the doorway. She smiles, then passes the flask to our daughter, who looks up at me and grins from ear to ear. She jumps off her stool, one she chose especially because it goes up and down. Our daughter hugs my legs and stands on her tiptoes for a kiss.

A kiss for my favourite girl.

A kiss for my favourite Daddy.

I'm tired. I feel like I can't remember the last time I had some sleep; my body is slow and unresponsive. The breakfast is nice. Natural yoghurt and muesli followed by poached egg on toast and a cup of mint tea. Marie says that too much caffeine can cause sleepless nights and that mint and green teas are better for hydration and digestion. I don't mind really. With or without caffeine I haven't been sleeping, so what does that mean? When I've made this point to Marie she tells me that I sleep like a baby. A baby? Am I not always awake at night then? Marie must be thinking of someone else.

Our daughter has jumped from her stool again and is clinging to my leg. She is squeezing it tight, as she does every morning, grinning at me and leaving kiss shaped saliva marks on the knee of my trousers.

Without looking at me, our daughter jumps back onto her stool and finishes her breakfast. I'm watching her concentrating on putting the spoon up to her mouth so as not to spill any milk on the tabletop. She has the spoon in a contorted, twisted position that is doubling her probable lack of success. Marie said that these things sort themselves out in time and we shouldn't be concerned. I am concerned. I have every right to wonder why, at the age of six, our daughter finds it almost impossible to hold her fucking spoon properly. A cheeky giggle escapes from the gap-toothed mouth that is eventually managing to eat cornflakes as Marie asks me, in a singsong manner, what I'm looking at. I say to her that can't a father look at his daughter if he wants to, and I smile at both of them.

I am Daddy. I want to devour Little Red Riding Hood.

I finish the tea and pick up my keys and my briefcase. Today I am travelling to work on the train. Twice this week I will use the trains so that Marie can drop our daughter off at school and attend to all her chores like shopping and meeting friends. On those other days some friends do the drop off and pick up. One week it's two days, the next it's three and then back to two. They alternate the drop off and pick up regime. I don't always keep track of the timetable and a few weeks ago I had to travel on the train at very short notice. I can't say I was happy about it, but it was my mistake, wearily accepted. I had a presentation and, well, it didn't go very well because I thought I had the car and was going to drive to work, but I have to catch the train earlier than I usually leave the house to get to work and it arrives later than when I drive to work. I had to catch the next train, which I only just caught, and I arrived thirty-three minutes after I was supposed to have started the presentation. I did my best but I knew it was frowned upon. I didn't really have an interesting excuse or a convenient reason why I hadn't phoned; why I was actually late. The bosses were sympathetic in that disappointed way people are when you know they will laugh at you later for your miserable incompetence. Of course I understand the importance of routine, it's just that I can tend to lose track when my workload is heavy, and what with the sleep issue and the way my thoughts race at night, I find that I tend to lose track of the routine and timetable.

I don't think I've always been like this. Some part of me tries to suggest that it used to be different; it used to be easier to exist. Not this, not this tired shell and mind that struggles to deal with the everyday things one has to contend with. Something else, something less tightly wound. No, that's not quite right. Less tight. I feel like my skin is too tight and it is squeezing me. Ironic then, that the actual skin itself is not tight and elastic, but loose, certainly looser than last year, and this makes me think that perhaps the tightness is under my skin, like this loose skin is a suit. A suit of skin. I realise how ridiculous this sounds. Of course it's absurd. What am I thinking?

I wonder if when I have this sort of… speculation, whether other people think these things as well. It's that thought that justifies my continued, it's not quite like this, but my continued indulgence in these thoughts. They've been steadily building over the last couple of years. I don't know where they're coming from, and I can't particularly put my finger on the exact source, but the frequency is increasing, and if I am to be honest, I like it. I don't think I've ever admitted it before.

Marie prods me. Our daughter laughs from her up-and-down stool. I kiss Marie on the forehead and jangle my keys as I head for the door. There's a bye that hangs in the air as I close the door behind me, using the key to turn the lock quietly instead of slamming it shut. I stand on our doorstep looking at the rain pouring down. A hat. What if I bought myself a nice hat like my father used to wear when it was the regulation fashion accessory of the sincerely middle aged? It's hardly worth the expense considering the thinning head of hair I now have.

I catch my reflection in the side window of a car. The rain is splashing and streaking down the glass. Distorted and caricatured, I wonder if this is how I really look. If this thing, this sad, sad creature I see before me, is my true image; a confession of some sort… I really ought to have brought an umbrella. The rain is coming down quite hard now, and I still have a fair way to walk to the train station.

The train is late. I am going to be late. I don't mind. Really, I don't mind in the slightest. As people fought to get on, their wet, damp bodies pushing closely together, the drips from their noses and chins falling onto the free newspaper everyone just has to pick up, I waited. I waited and still managed to get on without fuss or desperation. I'm quite relaxed in these circumstances. I have much more important things to think about than soggy newspapers and stuffy train carriages.

A young woman, with pretty eyes and a mouth you would let yourself be completely consumed by, unintentionally brushes her breast against me. She doesn't even apologise. Did she not feel me? Am I invisible? If I brushed against her, what would she feel? What would she… Nothing. It would be nothing. No one feels anything anymore, contained as they are in their own shallow self-satisfied existence. I'd like to kiss that young woman, just to see what this new vacuousness tastes like, to feel that thick mouth on mine…

I really must stop right there.

She would feel something now if I brushed against her.

It's nearly time. The final stop approaches and everyone is getting anxious, getting ready to run to work. This train terminates here. I'm tired. I'm not running anywhere. Not running to anything.

I'm late today because I didn't have the car. And they'll look at me and roll their eyes when I get to the office, and I'll apologise and suffer the temporary condescension. Everyone has to catch a train to work, they will say. But mine was late and today I don't have the car, I'll reply. That's no excuse, they will say. But it's all right, I'll tell them. I won't be travelling by train tomorrow. I'll be taking the car to work.

And perhaps tomorrow, I won't be driving it back.

Red

Roelof Bakker

Already late for work, she's stopped in her tracks by a tempting window display. BRINGING LIFE TO TECHNOLOGY. A carefully selected line up of consumer goods. She sees a kettle, a toaster, a juicer, a liquidizer, a hoover, a cooker, a cappuccino maker and a laptop.

Every product exudes luxury. They're calling out at her through the glass window, intent on hypnotizing her purse. They all share a colour. Each available in the same sophisticated deep red: the red of a fine Bordeaux, Tom Ford Cherry Lush Lipstick, gushing blood.

The woman stares, trance-like, then starts to laugh hysterically. Tears stream down her face. She's in stitches. It's hurting.

Passers-by look at her with disdain and surprise. They can see she's smartly dressed. She's beautiful. She looks normal, just like them. She's not a tramp, that's for sure. Mad?

Two shop assistants are watching her, from behind the window. Should they call the police? Can someone be arrested for hysterical behaviour outside a shop?

The laughter stops. The woman pulls herself together. Re-arranges her hair. Flattens her skirt. Clutches her bag. Makes a firm decision.

Lillywhites. Buy a baseball bat. This is important. Go.

Oh, and fuck work. She was supposed to be in that dreaded meeting half an hour ago. Best switch off her phone; ignore any messages from her PA.

She's back at the store an hour later. BRINGING LIFE TO TECHNOLOGY. What a load of bollocks. Who comes up with these ridiculous slogans?

All this stuff, admittedly, looks gorgeous. The red is very appealing. But let's be honest. It's all doomed. Give it a few weeks and these things will be worn, scratched, tatty and used up. Start to malfunction, give up life altogether.

She steps into the store. Smiles at the young shop assistant positioned in the entrance doing her meet-and-greet routine. She pushes over the cooker. Grabs the upright hoover. Smashes it into the laptop. Topples the juicer.

She whisks the baseball bat out of the Lillywhites carrier and takes care of the rest of the display. Product murder. Just smash, no grab. BRINGING DEATH TO TECHNOLOGY. All these items now have no life at all.

The kettle will never boil.
The toaster will never toast.
The juicer will refuse to juice.
Not a drop of liquid from the liquidizer.
The hoover won't do any hoovering.
The cooker's crooked.
No froth from the cappuccino maker.
The laptop's topped.

All lies, lies, lies, dirty stinking lies, she shouts. Kill the lies, kill the lies!

The police are on their way, instructed that no one should approach this dangerous woman. The manager has overseen the evacuation of shoppers and shop assistants. A crowd has gathered outside. The manager, at a safe distance, is trying to talk sense into the woman, asking her calmly to put the bat down. She tells him to shut the fuck up or he might regret ever having spoken to her.

She's not done. With her newly discovered strength, she sees no reason why she can't smash her way through the reinforced safety shop window glass. She slams away with the baseball bat. Soon a crack appears. Result.

It's unlikely she'll be able to destroy the whole window, but a hole will do. She's only trying to make a point after all. She batters away to create a succession of cracks roughly following the outline of her body. Hits with the bat furiously until the glass begins to give.

She takes a few steps back and with unexpected force lunges the side of her body into the weakened section of glass, which smashes onto the pavement. The woman is hurled along with it to the other side of the shop window, almost into the crowd, who move back, petrified.

No sign of the police.

Sweat pours down her forehead, her hair's a mess, her clothes are disheveled. There are scratches on her legs, her elbows and her arms. Her hands are filthy. There's blood to the side of her head. She doesn't know. She doesn't care. She feels happy and free. Like a winner. She's achieved what she set out to do. She had the same ecstatic feeling when she won the swimming competition at school when she was twelve. She was good at the front crawl. Still is. Her dad was so proud.

She looks up at the people on the pavement. It's as if they're cheering and clapping and everyone is taking photographs to record her moment of triumph, her protest of consumer discontent.

She bows, then withdraws into the shop through the gap she's created. As she turns her body, the top of her thigh pushes into the sharp edge of the remaining glass. It cuts through her pale blue cotton skirt and the Agent Provocateur frilly knickers. It pierces her skin. Cuts deep into her femoral artery.

A Writer Tries To Work It Out

Jose Varghese

True Love

Ajjay was for all reasons a perfect gentleman – it's just that he thought his voice was perfect for karaoke nights. His audience often squirmed in the self-loathe of the choiceless. They punished themselves with song after song delivered in high fidelity – in the croakiest of voices, striking off-key every now and then. Let's face it – he was a horrible singer. But his customers had to go through his 'Friday Nights at Lakeview Restaurant' with the bizarre experience of shoving tasty food into their mouth and straining to speak with their companions, amidst the loud music. He ran the restaurant, which was in central Mumbai, and it was his idea that his talent could be showcased on Fridays there, since no one else in town so far had the good taste to identify the singer in him. Those who knew about the Friday Nights and didn't care much for the tastiest food around would avoid it. But those who were addicted to the aroma and taste of the food served there (thanks to his wonderful chef Senoy) would let themselves go through the debacle, and say that life happens this way - that it's often a mixture of the incredibly good and the intolerably bad elements.

His taste in music was strange as well. On some nights he would chase the unlikely bunch of Depeche Mode, Aerosmith, David Bowie, The Black Keys, Arctic Monkeys, Darren Hayes, Michael Bolton and Mark Knopfler, often mistaking the voice and style of one for the other, and failing miserably to imitate all those falsettos and vibratos. On some other nights, he would sing ghazals – Jagjith Singh, Ghulam Ali, Anoop Jalota, Manhar Udhas and the like. He used to sing in female voice as well, but he stopped that on his own, after he found himself capable of releasing just air through his mouth instead of any voice after a night full of singing like Noor Jehan, Salma Agha and Iqbal Bano. He didn't want to ruin his vocal chords. They were precious, to him. And there were nights when he would sing away the popular and notorious Hindi film songs. He had a special liking for Sonu Nigam, Kishore Kumar and K.J Yesudas. And he brought an end to the respect his listeners ever had for the wonderful songs sung by them. They even started to forget that those were songs once, after listening to Ajjay.

*

'Well, I think you are trying to tell your readers a lot about your character here, Vivek. And you may bore them with the names of all those singers. It also makes you a bit showy. I don't see any scope for dialogue here in the near future. It will be almost like a Russian novel sans the seriousness.'

'Yes Julie, Russian novels – that's my vision. Just recently I heard an established writer saying that modern Indian English fiction is full of dialogues, which takes away the seriousness of the narrative. I'm all for Russian literature, especially of the late Nineteenth Century. That's where Indian Literature has to look up to. And you are mistaken about seriousness. I am damn serious about this writing. Even humour can be approached seriously, you see.'

'But there could be a few dialogues here and there. Crisp, convincing ones.'

'I'll think about it. But it's my story. So I will do whatever I feel like doing with it.'

'Then why did you show it to me? I thought it was because you cared for my opinion.'

'Of course, I care for it. Now, let's change the subject, before our entire conversation ceases to be crisp and convincing.'

'Ah ha! You beat me there. Let's just walk a little more. I love this beach a lot. It's not at all touristy. It's so calm here.'

'Why do you like to walk when you have a lot to talk about?'

'Who told you that I have a lot to talk about?'

'It's a guess. Am I not right?'

'Not at all.'

'Then I guess we'll just walk, as usual, in silence, after an argument.'

*

True Love – continued

Ajjay was thirty-two years old, and though he had fallen in love a few times and everything felt perfect while he was in it, he never got married. But then, on a Friday Night, he saw a girl sitting alone in a table for two and listening to his song intently. He thought she was in love with his singing, as everyone else. She was trying the famous seafood combo in his restaurant, and was enjoying it for sure. Since she didn't have anyone with her, she tried to focus on the singing, and was at a loss. She was in the same predicament as with those around her. She wanted to have her food, and couldn't run away from the place just because of the horrible songs. So she just tried to keep a straight face and tried so hard to focus on the taste of what she was eating.

Ajjay went to her table after the singing. He gave chance to new singers among his customers. Those who were desperate and in love with their own voice would sing in the intervals during which he tried to interact with his customers. They were kind to him, thanks to Senoy.

'Hello Madam, are you enjoying the food? I am Ajjay.'

'Oh yes, very much. And your singing too. I am Gita.'

And they started talking. Despite his bad singing, Ajjay was a charm-

er. She thought he looked like the Spanish actor Sergi Lopez, and he could find in her a similarity to Juliette Binoche. So it was almost like a crazy casting of an ambitious movie about a transnational affair, hot and sensual from the very beginning. But no, there were more things to it than that. She told him gently that he may do better if he just played the original songs, since she was not a great fan of karaoke. This hurt him a lot. It was the first that someone was being so painfully honest with him. But on an afterthought, he liked her honesty. He said he was determined not to stop singing, ever. Because it meant a lot to him. It meant everything. He knew that he was better than the best, and that was enough. She could just laugh aloud at this. In fact, she liked his honesty and the aggressiveness in his argument. She said she would come there again, but not again on a Friday night. That was settled.

And a few weeks later, they decided to get intimate. This meant that they were ready for getting involved, physically. And it went well. Everything was perfect. Ajjay was not allowed to sing, but he could talk about music. He didn't mind it. He had his fans waiting for him on Fridays. He just had to separate his music from his love.

Senoy remained in the background all this while. But one day, Gita asked him about his chef, and he told her about Senoy. She was from Thailand, but settled comfortably in Mumbai for such a long time. She was in her forties, and a spinster. Gita wanted to see her and thank her for the wonderful food. He liked the idea and in no time he arranged a meeting between the two. The two women got along well and in a few weeks' time Ajjay started feeling that everything was not so perfect between him and Gita. There was a distance that could not be ignored. He couldn't find out for what exact reasons she was growing so distant. And one day, he got a letter from Senoy – saying that she was leaving for Thailand. It was a resignation letter as well. She was happy in Mumbai, but was sad as well. Now she is not sad. She can be happy anywhere in the world, because she was taking Gita with her to Thailand.

*

'I like the twist there, Vivek. But still I have a problem with the descriptions. I strongly feel that there could be more dialogues.

You have just a pair of dialogues there, for the sake of it.'

'This story doesn't need dialogues. It's meant to be a small story, which can just be narrated.'

'Well, I felt that it ended abruptly. What looked like a lengthy Russian novel has just become a short short story now.'

'Well, you seem to know nothing about the postmodernist metafictional devices that suit the postcolonial appropriation and approbation...'

'Please do stop it, Vivek. You sound like a street-side magician.'

'It seems we should change the topic now. It's not a perfect idea to discuss my stories with you. But I am writing an auto-biographical story soon, which is rather lengthy. And it's full of dialogues. You may like it.'

'Let us see. Why don't we just go and sit somewhere? See there's some shade under that tree. And there's a bench there.'

'Great idea.'

*

Brothers

'*You have mistaken me brother, I told you that I am a poet. Shayar means poet.*'

'*Really? Oh yes, I get it now. So, you sing your own songs, or poems – whatever you call them?*'

'*Not really, brother. I do not set music to my poetry very often. I sing the ghazals of Jagjit Singh, Ghulam Ali and Mehdi Hassan, and – this may sound funny to you – I sing some of the ghazals by Iqbal Bano, Noor Jehan and the movie-ghazal versions of Ashaji and Lataji. Sometimes in my own voice and sometimes in female voice.*'

'Oh, I would really love to listen to your singing someday. But now, we have to find out where Talia Street is.'

'*Don't worry brother, I will find it for you. Though I am not a proper taxi driver, I can find my way round Jeddah. This street just happens to be the hangout place for rich kids – the kind who attend your university*'.

'*But I don't think all of them are rich, by the way. I found a few who* wore thawbs with threadbare collars, and some told me that they were different from the rich kids, and really needed some education for a job'.

'I see, but they are what we call exceptions. Just have a look at the number of cars in the parking lots of your university. I don't think that the majority of students in a Pakistani or Indian university will ever be able to afford such luxury cars.'

'That's true.'

I was beginning to drift off. And, I wanted to find out Talia Street and the Mobily telephone office pretty soon. I was stuck with a slow Internet connection. All my work, and communication with all those whom I cared for, were in jeopardy.

Then he started to sing. And how could I believe my ears! He sang so beautifully that I suddenly felt I could stop worrying about the torn, damp seats of the car with a faulty a/c and the bad odour attendant to it.

He sang of the lights switched on one by one in high-rise buildings and how the people in the streets could have looked like worms from above – if anyone bothered to look. But no one looked downwards from the glass windows. The shadows that played behind them were busy with the banalities of their life. They wouldn't know, wouldn't care, if anyone was killed in the streets, or died of hunger, of a bleeding throat after so many days of begging for food.

He wasn't singing of Jeddah, where I did not find anyone killed or dying in the streets in the two weeks I had been there. Or, perhaps, the sights escaped my eyes. But he was singing of the cities that bothered the modernist Indian/Pakistani poets, of the contrasts that were the life in streets there. He seemed to favour the idea that man was essentially lost in a concrete jungle where his own shadows lurched behind him like poisonous snakes.

'Oh brother, I guess we are lost.'

'Don't bother, keep singing.'

'But… we need to find the way back too, eh? I have to confess that I'd never been to this particular place before, and I need your help to get directions. These shops look too big, and the people over there seem educated enough to understand your English…'

We had a real ride that day, but I managed to make him sing all the way back. In the short intervals he spoke of his cousin who was participating in a Pakistani reality show on TV that featured unknown singers from the rural areas of the country. He said that his cousin had a voice that could make anyone sit back and listen.

We stopped by an Indian restaurant in Sharafiya Street, where he accepted my invitation to be my guest and tried the South Indian dishes I suggested. He told me about his family which was displaced during the Partition when the two countries – India and Pakistan – were formed as an aftermath of the end of British colonialism in the subcontinent. He spoke of the way his family had to leave behind their business in the north of India and travel in bullock-carts in the night, fearing death every minute, to their new nation. A saga of displacements, from the days of prosperity in a familiar land that suddenly turned hostile, to a new land of confusions. Endless days of struggle, disenchantment and the sudden realization that they were thrown into irredeemable poverty in the process. Another journey to the holy land, for sustenance. More struggles, some luck. A wife who failed to bear him children till she was 42. A journey to Makkah. A chance meeting with an expert doctor in Jeddah, and a miracle that ensued. A daughter, who shines like a piece of moon. All due to the grace of God.

'Brother, I am not too religious anyway. I just acknowledge a miracle when it comes my way. I let my experiences guide me, and I call you 'brother' in the true spirit of the word, though you happen to be a Christian from India.'

'Hmm... that's a touchy topic. But I'm always lucky to find friends who think like this. My best friend in the university happens to be from Tunisia, and I guess we get along better than those who try to stick together on the basis of nationality or religion. After all, we are all here with a fair share of burdens and the need to work towards economic stability, and I don't find any reason for hostility'.

'You are right, but it doesn't take much time to lose common grounds for friendship. I remember the open hostility between Indians and Pakistanis in the streets at the time when the Kargil War was going on. Even recently, one of my Indian friends told me about the sudden change in the attitudes of his fellow-employees when India accused Pakistan for the Taj Hotel attacks. '

'It seems funny that there is indeed scope for Indo-Pakistan confronta-

tions in Saudi Arabia.'

'But my brother, I am for peace, and love, and music. May I sing another ghazal for you?'

And he sang again. Then I requested him to sing a ghazal of Jagjit Singh which he thought was too gloomy for the occasion but obliged in the spirit of friendship. Then it was time for some surprise, as he sang in beautiful female voice, a song by Lata Mangeshkar. As we approached the road to my apartment, he tried to impress me by reciting 'Our Father in Heaven' and 'Hail Mary'. His father was educated in a missionary school in India, and he passed on these prayers to his children as exercises in English. I told him that this convinced me of the secular liberal outlook of his family. But there was no need for any such evidence to find a true friend in him.

*

'This sounds more interesting. To be honest, I can't bear with your intellectual observations, but this seems to have a story-line. And there is some overlap between the first story and this one, regarding music. Are you going to develop it further?'

'Not exactly. This story will be in three parts. There will a second part, which involves a colleague in the university where I worked for a while. And the third part will be with someone I had a casual language exchange deal.'

'It sounds interesting.'

'Julie, are you pretending to encourage me? Are you really beginning to get bored with me and my writings?'

'Why such a doubt?'

'No, I just feel I am not listening to you much these days.'

'That's fine. One day I might really speak up, and you may just make it into a story.'

'That's a good proposition!'

'Wait for the day.'

'I will.'

*

Brothers - continued

'It's time for a cup of coffee and a cigarette now. Would you like to join me?'

'Of course, but please do keep the one meter distance between us when you smoke, and don't blow the smoke in my direction'

'Come on brother, these are very mild cigarettes, the ones women would smoke. I am waiting for the Tunisian cigarettes my wife has promised to send me through a relative. Did I tell you that she and my son will come here for the vacation?'

'Really? Is your son old enough to travel?'

'He is nearly three years now. Old enough to repeat the anti-smoking slogan in Tunisian TV channels. I had an argument with my wife when she made him say that to me over the phone.'

'But why?'

'Because that's not the way a son should be taught to behave. He should learn to respect his father.'

'But he has the right to care for his father's health too.'

'I took X-rays for the visa. My lungs are clear. I don't have any health problem. But no, let's not talk about this. A man has the right to enjoy his cup of coffee and cigarette in peace.'

'Okay. But I would like to tell you something interesting. I had this monitoring job in a class recently, and my companion for the job was Ezeddin, your countryman. One boy made a presentation about smoking, and Ezeddin asked a few questions and said in the end that he hates smoking, and the people who smoke.'

'Did he really say that? It's disgusting.'

'Even I was shocked to hear that. You see, I will never be able to say that, because my father was a heavy smoker. And many of my friends happen to be smokers. But you are the only one who gets the privilege to smoke in my company'

'Thank you. This means a lot to me.'

'Are you joking?'

'No. I was really hurt when my son tried to intimidate me.'

'Come on, he had no clue on what he was saying.'

'But it hurts.'

'OK, smoke on. Let's talk about something else.'

'Do I sound like a fool to you? Hey don't laugh at me.'

'But you are laughing too'.

'Hey, have a look at this mobile video. It's my son playing with his plastic football on the day I left for Jeddah.'

'He's so tiny.'

'Just two and a half years old, but a stubborn boy.'

'Don't be tough on him.'

'No, you know I love him. He is my first son. I asked him to give me the ball, but he didn't.'

'You were a fool to ask for it. I can see how much the ball means to him.'

'But I am his father. He should respect me, right? I needed to keep it as a token from him.'

'You make me laugh again.'

'Really? Am I too silly?'

'Yes, I am afraid. I used to think of chain-smokers as toughies.'

'I am a toughie.'

'You have time for a story?'

'Yes, ten minutes more for my class, have time for two more cigarette.s'

'You are burning your lips.'

'Let them burn. What's the story?'

'Did I tell you about the Pakistani friend?'

'Shehzad? The taxi driver who sings?'

'Yes. He was not a taxi driver. He just happened to have a car. His job was to deliver bakery items to the minimarkets.'

'I see. I know so many of them like that. They make some extra Riyals with their car when they are free.'

'Exactly. He was supposed to leave Saudi for good yesterday. I wanted to record some of his songs. He showed me all his poetry – written in paper napkins, hotel bills and notebooks discarded by students. I never imagined he lived in a room with five others.'

'Did you go to his room?'

'Yes, he invited me there. He was waiting there with his friends with a

1.5 litre bottle of Mirinda.'

'But do you have to accept the invitation by everyone? People can be harmful, you know.'

'But not this one.'

'How do you know?'

'Because he is a singer with a heavenly voice.'

'You are crazy.'

'He showed me the photos of his wife and his little daughter. She was very cute, with a miraculous smile.'

'The worst part of working in a place like this is to leave your children behind and miss the process of their growing up.'

'I wanted to scan his poems to my laptop. I was unable to read Urdu, but wanted to show them to my friends who could. I couldn't do anything which I wanted to do, except giving him a pack of sweets for his daughter.'

'What happened?'

'Some native citizen hit his car near the bridge. The car was 'gifted' to him by an Indian friend, and he didn't have proper papers. He was arrested and taken to the police station. His friends told me about this yesterday. They said that his work visa was also expired. No one knows how to contact him. His flight must have left yesterday, without him.'

'It's better not to think, brother, of things that hurt. It's time for my class. Let me have one more puff… drink it to the lees!'

*

'...'

'What do you think about this Julie?'

'Do you really care for what I think about this?'

'Yes, of course.'

'Look Vivek, I'm not in a mood to talk with you today.'

'Then why did you agree to meet me here today?'

'We always end up talking about your world. Your stories… you know what Vivek, you are so full of yourself.'

'I thought you always wanted to do that. You wanted to see my writing, to discuss the things I narrate.'

'But you don't pay any attention to what I say.'

'Julie, you can only express your responses, you can't influence a writer beyond a point.'

'I know that now. But what about our personal lives?'

'What about that?'

'You seem not to care about me, Vivek. You are so much engrossed in the world of your characters that you tend to ignore my concerns.'

'What concerns?'

'Enough, Vivek. Let's stop there. By the way I like your colleague in the story; he's better than you.'

*

Brothers - continued

'It's Mithat, your Turkish friend. Please open the door, brother.'

'Yes, come in.'

'I am bringing too much lessons today, brother. Too many practice in car. My English perfect now, eh?'

'Almost, if you could get the 'too much' and 'too many' out of your sentences.'

'Okay brother, I am trying too much. Sorry. I am trying.'

'You have a new uniform?'

'No uniform. I design this. Company symbol red. I made shirt and pants red. How it look?'

'It looks good, but where is your tie?'

'The police took tie. And the pen drive we bought. 16 GB. You remember? Police took everything.'

'The police caught you?'

'Yes, they catch me last week. Crazy customer said I try to steal car. He did not pay tax and left car near my office and said I steal car. Police take me. My wife and children worry, no news for two days.'

'Oh sorry. I didn't know it.'

'You will not know it. My mobile in police station now, with belt, tie, pen drive, you know 16 GB. Costly one we bought with discount.'

'Yes, we bought similar ones. Will you get them back?'

41

'I try, but don't know. See, they hit too much on arm and face this side'

'Oh dear, it looks bad. Did you see a doctor?'

'No need for doctor. I am fine. Two days, it is gone.'

'Please do come in and take a seat. You need some juice?'

'Yes, thanks. I like orange juice.'

'Okay, in a minute.'

'Are you packing? Going home?'

'Yes, I am leaving this place, forever.'

'Why?!'

'My contract is not renewed for next year.'

'Too much sad news. So, you are leaving?'

'Yes, I have to leave now, there is no other choice.'

'What about Tunisian friend Moath? He was worried, calling you evenings, discussing things…'

'Glad news is that Moath's contract is renewed. Poor guy, he was under real pressure. He needs to stay here for at least five years in order to build a house and so on…'

'Good. But I am sad brother. What will you do?'

'I have some offers in India. In fact it is a blessing in disguise. I need to stay there for some more days to finish my research work and get a government job…'

'But they don't pay too much salary yes? Your job here good yes?'

'Yes, the job here was well paid, but I was not very happy here you know. I was feeling empty here.'

'What do you mean empty?'

'I don't know how to explain it. Just don't feel good.'

'You were feeling sad? What reason? Girl friend in India?'

'Nothing like that, hehe. May be I am just crazy.'

'Yes, you crazy, but good man, brother. Now, who will teach me English? And, you never learn Arabic, always practising Spanish.'

'I am so sorry Mithat. I wanted to learn Arabic first, but then I lost interest in it. But I guess I am a better teacher than a student. Your English is almost perfect now.'

'I want to be university teacher like you some day. They pay too much, eh? Everything is possible. I learn Arabic first and can read Quran better than Saudi people now. I become English teacher in five years.'

'Yes, it's possible Mithat. You may need to get some degrees though.'

'I don't know. May be some degree, diploma for people like me. I did not complete school.'

'Let us see, if a car mechanic from Turkey can become a body shop assistant manager in Jeddah, everything is possible.'

'Not now brother, assistant manager in the future.'

'Soon, very soon.'

'You no writing now? No story about people here?

'Oh, I am getting lazy these days. I just listen to people.'

'Brother, you crazy because you carry too much story inside.'

'You are right, perhaps'.

'I am sad brother, when you leaving?'

'Next week.'

'You have shopping? I have car downstairs. We can go to Hyper Panda, but first near mosque to buy cheap vegetables and eggs for my home.'

'Sure.'

'I need pen drive new'.

'Okay we can have a look. But no need to buy a tie. I have some which were never used. I won't need them in India.'

'Thank you brother, only if you don't need. I will drive you airport next week.'

'Thank you. I have some furniture which I may not be able to take home. Would you like to have them? This big table for instance?'

'Brother, first we try sell them second hand people.'

'Okay, but I'm afraid we don't have much time for everything. I would like it if you find some use for them.'

'I am sad, you leaving so fast. Don't worry about furniture, I will try sell and get some money for you. If no selling, I will take it. Will take my oldest son Emir to help me take it.'

'Great. So, let's go shopping now.'

'Of course. I will show you place to get real cheap pyjamas, half length, full length, real cheap.'

'Okay, I am ready.'

*

Finale

We were so full of love that it kept us up in the air, like the balloons someone tied on the tree stump. Well, that's what I thought when we sat down on the heart-shaped rock on the top of the mountain. It was not easy for her to climb all the way up from where the buses stopped, but once we were there all on our own, she started to relax. I took in the beautiful sight far below where everything looked small enough to create the feel of a painting – acrylic or oil on canvas. There was hardly any movement there. I felt elated. A perfect setting for two people to be together.

Then there was a moment of doubt, and I knew she was fighting back memories, as her trembling hand reached out for mine.

Life from such an altitude felt good to me...it was like being a part of the world beyond pain, and frustration. But I was worried about her at the same time. Though it felt good to be there for her at the moment, I was waiting for her to open up, to reveal her true feelings, to wipe away her past that stood between us.

'It's been a long time since I thought of talking to you...' she started.

'Please do talk Julie. The silence doesn't feel like gold to me.' I tried to humour her.

But she didn't smile with me. I felt stupid the way I did many times when she used that emotional high ground against me. I looked away. Sensing my discomfort, she squeezed my hand.

'Look here Vivek, I know you are a good person. I trust you. But you will never be able to understand the mess I am.'

'There you go again! Why do you expect anyone to understand anyone else? See, I don't even understand myself at times.'

'That's not what I mean. Don't take this lightly. If we go on like this, hoping to live together, we will reach a phase where we won't be able to connect with each other. It's not your fault...', she paused.

'Whatever it is, you have to speak it out. This is really getting on my nerves', I said, a bit agitated.

She looked up with some hurt in her eyes and went back to her silence. I put my arm around her, liking it a bit that my words can hurt her and a kind gesture afterwards can perhaps make her feel better. She didn't respond.

'Julie, speak out.'

'Well, you must know that I lost my parents and my sister to a beautiful sight like this. The accident that took them away from me happened on a holiday. I stayed back in the boarding school, preparing for an exam.' She paused to drink a mouthful of water from the bottle we carried.

'They took me to the site, where my Dad's car was found almost at the bottom of the mountain, unrecognizable. And their bodies were still in it; not one of them in one piece.'

It shocked me that she told this deadpan, in a monotone. It was my turn now to weigh the discomfort of silence as she stared at me victoriously.

'I know you have a lot of romantic notions, but it's not going to work, Vivek.'

'But why not? Are you going to carry on like this – punishing yourself for not being dead with them?'

'You don't understand how insensitive you are Vivek', she withdrew her hand from mine. 'And that's why I know this is not going to work.'

I thought she was right. She had this immense capability to make me feel frustrated beyond any limit. Perhaps it was not worth struggling for this, I thought.

'May be you are right', I said. 'But I'm not sure you're going to stay like this forever. You're going to find someone who...'

'That shouldn't bother you. Unless you need to justify yourself...'

'Justify myself? For what? I don't know what you mean.'

'I know what I mean. But only you know for what. Why should you bother about my future, with or without someone? We are just not going to be together. That's the end of it.'

I started feeling so bad that I felt like pushing her down

from the rock. After all, she will feel good to be dead, with her good for nothing, non-existent family. There are prettier girls out there, with less complicated minds...

Oh no, is this me thinking? How mean of me... She is right. I'm not the one for her, or perhaps I'm not the one for anyone...

I looked into her eyes, and thought she was smiling at me. It seemed she was able to read my mind. There was no sadness in her eyes.

'Why did you choose me, Vivek?'

'What? I don't get you.'

'I'm asking – why did you choose me, out of all the girls you knew?'

'Because you were different... well, you had something special in you.'

'Listen to yourself. You are speaking in clichés. I will give you the answer to my question. You chose me because you thought there was less to hate in me than in the other girls. Also because you thought I was less demanding and more pleasing than...'

'Stop it, Julie. You are talking nonsense.'

'No, I'm talking sense. It's you who were thinking nonsense all the way.'

'Well... if you knew this all the way, why did you get close to me?'

'I didn't get close to you.'

'What? So, all those times we spent together meant nothing to you? Were you just acting it... cheating me?'

'Don't get upset, Vivek. I spent time with you just because I felt good about it then. Can't two people spend some time together happily, and still not get 'close', as you say?'

'You are confusing me.'

'It's not me – it's all those books that you read, and those movies that you watch, and those people with whom you spend your time that confuses you.'

'I don't understand you Julie.'

'That's not my fault. You see, I can't do anything about this. And I was trying to tell you that it was not your fault that you don't understand me. We are just two different people who can perhaps spend some friendly moments together. Don't try to draw me into your daydreams. I am someone in flesh and blood, and I'm different, yes, different, from what you think.'

I found it difficult to talk, and once again fought the temptation to push her down the rock. Why did I take so much trouble to come all this way with her? Why did I fail to see her problems before I let this develop so far?

'Julie, you are trying to be more sophisticated than you are. Perhaps you got the idea from the books you read, and…'

'Exactly. You've got a point there. We experience life differently.'

'But don't they say that opposites attract? Can't we have the differences and still be in love?'

'Oh, not again. I really can't stand these clichés.'

'Julie, we all speak in clichés, don't we? I am not ashamed of saying things that had been said earlier by someone else. I don't think there's anything that comes from vacuum to make us sound more intelligent than the rest. Our words come out of our limited experiences in life.'

'I won't counter that, if we are going to have a debate. My point is that we are people with different experiences and points of view, and we don't necessarily have to be attracted to each other just because we are the opposites, if you like.'

'You knew this from the beginning? Then why didn't you discourage me?'

'Discourage you from what?'

'From loving you.'

'Do you love me?'

I fell silent. It's no use talking to her. She's right, I thought. How could I love her?

'Vivek, you just think it's not romantic to answer the question, but I know your answer. It's not that I cannot connect with people. But I'm sick of your quick solutions. You think forgetting is a means of survival, but for me it's the height of insensitivity. It's ingratitude to life.'

I gaped in disbelief at her eloquence, as I tried in vain to decipher her thoughts. This girl is too much for me, I decided.

'Vivek, I don't want you to be cured of your optimism. May be things work for you that way. But for me, life doesn't work that way.'

She stood up. I sat there for a moment, unable to see things clearly. The beautiful valley was there. I knew that it existed, like me, but it looked blurry now. Was it my confusion, or my eyes, or the darkness that fell like a blanket… oh no, I'm thinking in clichés.

'Vivek, get up. Let's make a move,' she said.

The Regular

Mark Mayes

One

The snow had almost gone. Patches of greying slush remained in the gutters, on the traffic islands, on the bus-stop roof. An elderly woman wearing a pink scarf began to cross the road below my window. She took her time did this one. A blue hatchback car had to brake suddenly to avoid hitting her. She paid no attention to it at all, and continued to the pavement and out of my area of sight.

I replayed the scene I'd just witnessed, but this time the car, travelling much faster than originally, hit the elderly woman, crashing into her legs, upending her, and sending her rag-doll body and defenceless face slamming into and then crashing through the car's windscreen. Her thin legs spread out across the bonnet, a single black shoe left in the road. After a few seconds, the car drove off at a steadier pace, with the old woman stuck through the front window.

I smiled, and the smile went. I sipped the lemony wine. I tried to empty myself into the simple but discouraging act of purely being a middle-aged man, named Rodney, sitting alone with a bottle of white wine, in a cut-price chain-pub in Gloucester, on a winter's Wednesday afternoon.

And then, like a conjuring trick, he was there. A neatly bearded man, tall, in his fifties, grey felt hat in the Russian style, dark checked coat. This man had sat, without even asking if I minded, at my table, on the chair across from me. He looked out my window as if I didn't exist, as if I never had. In fact, he gave no suggestion that he even recognised that anyone else *was* at the table.

I glanced around the bar. There were several empty spots he could have sat at; admittedly no window tables were free, but still. Behind us a large television mutely flashed news images of an earthquake. I saw black faces in the rubble, and I turned away. What was it to do with me?

What I was more interested in was the precise nature of this interloper's game. In his bony, long-fingered hand he cupped a small liqueur glass that contained a thick greenish liquid. He cradled it like a talisman, all the time gazing down at the street below, then at the stained and flaking buildings opposite, with their blank windows. The large empty shop windows at street level, shops that had moved or gone bust. The vacancy.

I watched his face in profile. I took a drink and moved my bottle further into my half of the table. Just enough so he'd get the message. Not a flicker on that impassive side-on face. I could have moved. Yes, of course I could have. But why give him the satisfaction? Why must it always be me that has to move? I was waiting, you see. Waiting for him to do or say something. And that expectation held me glued to my chair.

His skin was olive, open-pored, but his features looked English, British or whatever. He was a mixture of sorts. That much I could tell.

Finally, I could bear the awkward presence of this man no longer without establishing most definitely that I was indeed a partner at the table. Had been, in fact, the original occupant.

I cleared my throat. A tiny muscle in his cheek twitched.

'Crème-de-Menthe?' I said.

He ignored me, his eyes lowered, studying the pavement below us; a pavement that I could see was empty. It was as if I hadn't spoken. I wondered for a little moment if I had in fact spoken, or had it only been at the level of a thought. Nothing registered in him. This was insulting, inhuman. And then I considered, was he deaf? Or perhaps brain-damaged in some way, autistic even. I drew the conclusion finally that he was more likely an ignorant so-and-so. One of a breed that were proliferating exponentially.

I took another swig of wine, which now tasted nasty and sour, rather than the pleasantly refreshing tartness it had before the man had sat down. Had this man changed the taste of my drink? My face grew hot with something I understood as repressed rage. 'Sind Sie blöd?' I whispered.

I remembered a little German from my Army years. Four of them, one willing German Fraulein, resulting in one cleft-palated baby boy, who was now a young man with a drug problem, apparently living in a squat on the outskirts of Hamburg. The Christmas cards and requests for money had stopped many years ago. Now all I was sent were intermittent hate-notes, forwarded on from my previous address. There might be a six-month gap, then the car-crash of her life, and my so-called son's was minutely served up to me on pink notepaper, in two languages, both barely legible. I had asked the man with the Russian hat if he was stupid. But again, did I really ask it, or had I only thought it?

Flyers on other tables advertised the 'Curry Club'. I'd removed the one before I'd sat down. To what extent, I wondered, was the purchasing of a curry in a pub on a certain day a token of actually belonging to a 'club'? The various members would have no independent or alternative way of recognising another member, other than seeing a tired-looking young woman (mostly) or man, some underperforming or drop-out student, I supposed, deliver the dish to a table in their view. And were there then furtive winks and knowing smiles between the curry-eaters, like some medium-spiced bunch of masons? Beyond the sharing of a similar food on a certain day, did the members meet up for other activities? Discussion groups, rambling, dogging-sessions? Were there founder or senior members? Initiation ceremonies? Could you be barred from full membership for some dodgy act with a poppadum?

Still he sat there. Ignoring me. Observing what out there? Couldn't he feel my eyes, my instant dislike of him? Not because of anything I knew about him, because I didn't know anything, but for his total disregard for my being in the world.

'You speak German?' he said, still looking out at the road. A large white van came tearing round the corner. I caught a flash of the logo on the side. Something like 'It's all done for you'.

His voice again was a mishmash, and deep, rich, like an actor's. I knew it wasn't simple English in his background. There was something foreign in there, but I would need to hear more.

'Ein bisschen,' I said, willing him to look at me. He didn't. I gazed over at the television screen. They were interviewing a floppy-haired, unnaturally tanned soap-star about his addiction revelations, i.e. a plug for his book. The soap star, who spoke and moved just like the character he played, was nodding like a nodding dog and producing a constant stream of psychobabble that the interviewer reflected back at him.

'And so in a sense I've finally come to terms with that primal sense of loss and abandonment. Addictive personalities are born not made, it's like its hard-wired, yeah?'

'This book you've written will surely be a wake-up call to the many young people trying these substances for the first time, thinking it could never be them, who might end up…'

'Well, that's right, yeah. I've been down that road and I feel a duty to tell of what I've seen. If I can help just one…'

I turned away and tuned out. He was staring at me, smiling. Right into my eyes. The nerve of it.

'Kowagaranaide,' he said.

'What?' I said.

'Don't be timid. Japanese.'

'What are you talking about? I was just sitting here minding my own…'

'Making cars crash into elderly women. Smashing their bones and faces. Shattered hips and jaws. Someone's mother, grandmother.'

'What the hell are you… how did you… ?' I put down my glass firmly, causing some wine to splash over the side. 'Look, pal, I suggest you find another table. I always sit here. You could have chosen any of those other tables,' I gestured around the room. 'Lots of room downstairs too.'

Now it was me who couldn't meet his eyes. I was shocked how he knew about my daydreaming. He'd seen right into me before he'd even arrived. I thought about leaving, or making a complaint to the manager, who I was on reasonable speaking terms with. But what had this strange bloke actually done to me? The manager would just advise me to sit somewhere else. But why should I? I was a regular!

He was Eastern European, I concluded, or possibly Czech, but had lived in England for some time. This was just guessing.

'What do you do for a living?' I asked him.

The smile vanished. He was studying me. He took a sip from the green liquid. It made him wince.

'Who are you talking to?' he said.

'To you. Who'd you think?'

'I think that you are a deeply unhappy man.' The smile flashed. One tooth was slightly off-colour. He resumed looking out the window.

'You can't say that,' I told him. 'You don't know me from Adam. What right have you got to come and sit down here and start getting in my head? Are you some sort of nutter?'

He began humming a tune. Deep and gravelly, coming from his chest. It sounded Hungarian or what I thought Hungarian music should sound like.

I refilled my glass, emptying the bottle. 'How did you know what I'd been thinking before? Go on, answer me.'

He emptied the little glass, wiped his mouth with the back

of his hand, and stood. I got a piny smell off him then. And a sort of mustiness, like some old churches. Giving me a sort of summing-up glance, he breathed in deeply, and said, 'It is not so hard to catch stray thoughts. Often the difficulty is keeping them away.'

'It's impossible. You're taking the piss.'

'So is pretending your son does not exist. Good day.' He gave me a little bow, which struck me as ridiculous.

'I didn't tell you anything about my son,' I shouted to his back as he went down the stairs. 'It's none of your bloody business!' A few people looked over. I didn't give a monkey's.

From the window, I saw him exit the pub and walk along the pavement. When he was level with my window, he looked up. Then he mouthed something that I couldn't make out. He might have actually said the words, but of course I couldn't hear. I watched his grey hat and long dark coat disappear.

Two

The next time I saw him was near the park. I sometimes go there to feed the ducks or read the newspaper on the bench if it's not too cold. I'd left the park itself and was heading back to my flat. I came to a crossroads that I didn't ever remember seeing before. I looked up one way, then the other on the bigger of the roads. The view didn't make sense. It didn't look like the town I lived in. I couldn't recognise anything, the buildings were the wrong colour and the wrong design. They came from a period I'd never seen before. And then I noticed the road signs. On all four signs of that crossroads it said The Park. The Park, The Park, The Park, The Park. That's crazy, I thought. I'm seeing things. I hadn't been drinking.

And then he appeared again, at my shoulder, like some big bearded parrot. Suddenly there, without any sense of his approach. He was dressed identically to that time in the pub.

'It's you,' I said.

'And it's you,' he said, smiling that unnerving smile, like he was looking down on me, humouring me. He was significantly taller than me as a matter of fact, and I'm never comfortable talking to very tall people. I feel like a little boy again. His eyes twinkled. There were actual sparks of light moving in them, and it wasn't a sunny day.

'Do you live around here?' I asked him.

'Oh, here or here abouts.'

I stepped back. I didn't wish to be too close. 'These flippin' signs,' I said, pointing at them. 'Some bugger's having a laugh. They all say the same thing.'

'Well, where do you want to go?' Again the piny smell came off him, and the mustiness. Perhaps the pinyness was covering an unwashed body.

'Home, where do you think?'

'Ah, home. We all want that, don't we? But home is not necessarily where we live, is it?'

'Hold on a minute. Don't start all that malarkey again. I remember that crack you made about my son. Who the hell are you? And what do you know about me?'

'Only what you wish to send out.'

'My thoughts are my own, geddit? My life is mine. I could get a restraining order on you, mate.'

'But I live here. It is you who is out of your territory.'

'This is *my* town. I've been here for years.'

'Your son needs you. He is falling through the cracks.'

'I never even got to know him properly. Never held him. She kept me away from all that. I've had no involvement in his life. He's not my…'

'Responsibility?'

'That's right. He's made whatever choices he made. Like we all have to.'

'Do you want to see him, Rodney?'

'How do you know my name? I never told you my name. Are you working for the police, or are you some kinda private detective? Has she hired you from Germany? I didn't think she cared enough.' I stepped further away, and turned to go down one of the roads named The Park. But which one could I choose? They all looked the same. Then it struck me: the view down each way of the two roads was the same. The same green gable on the house down each side of the larger road, the same arrangement of trees in the first few gardens. The cars, my God, the cars were the same. A green Nissan Micra. A white Peugeot. A white van on the other side, and the logo 'It's all done for YOU!' in swirly black letters on the side.

Then the other two The Park's: same cars here too, stretching as far as I could see. An identical cat nosing among some leaves at the foot of an identical tree about one hundred feet down each way.

'Take your pick,' he said. His eyes glinted more than before. He chuckled and shook his head mechanically from side to side like a seaside clown in a box.

'They're all the sodding same! What are you doing to the roads? This isn't where I live. I'm going home to my flat. I've got a microwavable cottage pie to eat. There's a film on I wanted to watch. I'm going home.'

'Then go,' he said.

All the strength went from my legs. I sank to my knees. I felt the cold and wet of the snow soak through the material. The arrangement of leaves on the ground was making me dizzy. There was a pattern in them and I was trying to work it out. Like seeing something in tea dregs or looking for Jesus in a funny-shaped vegetable. A solution lay in those leaves. I knew he was behind me.

'What should I do?' I said.

'Take your road.'

'To the park?'

'Where else?'

Three

After that park incident I shut down. I went to work as usual. I stayed in every night, watching the telly, reading the odd book. At weekends I might go to London for a change of air, or I might drive down to Bournemouth, as I had an old army mate there.

Steve was newly married and every time I'd go down they'd be having a blazing row. They'd expect me to umpire it. I'd sit with a can of something, trying to watch the football or whatever was on. 'Just try and be happy,' I told them. 'Just try and not let little things ruin the big picture.'

'What the fuck do you know about relationships?' Steve said. He was a bit pissed, but I could also see he was pissed off.

'What do you mean?' I said.

'I remember Inga, the way you treated her in front of us. Like a piece of *Scheisse*. You humiliated that girl,' he said. 'This German bint he had a kid with in Münster,' he explained to Kelly his fat wife. She shrugged, stuffed another sausage roll in her mouth. Steve had put on weight, too. He was fatter than her. They looked like male and female versions of each other.

'I didn't come down here for this,' I told him. I got up. He made a move. 'Don't think about it, mate,' I said.

'Fuck off, then, ponce,' he shouted when I was half way down the road. I realised then that our friendship was over. I realised at that moment that he was a very thick sort of individual. Not that I'm Einstein, but I've never really fitted in with the crowd, either in army life or my current job. I should have gone to a university or somewhere.

I stopped off at the services. It was dark, blustery, pleasantly lonely. I sat there with a stupidly priced bacon and egg sandwich and a mug of slosh. Two other people in the place. Why they have to have the lights up so bright, I don't know. I caught my reflection in the window and thought, no, that's not me.

I'd seen him as a baby. We tried making it work for a few months. I wondered what life held for him with a mouth like that, the cleft lip and palate, though I suppose they can do wonders these days. She stopped having sex with me so I looked elsewhere. I didn't feel any love for the boy, but I felt a curiosity and a kind of disgust that she and I had made him on one drunken night, with her mother snoring in the next room. I was sick after we did it. She woke up with my vomit in her hair. Who says romance is dead?

I tried not to think about what Steve had said. I'd never actually hit her, I knew that much.

An older couple were at a corner table. She stroked his lined face. He had his hand on hers. I found it hard to tear my eyes away. So it was possible.

Then I turned back to my sandwich and he was there. My shadow. Same hat and coat. Same neatly cut beard. Same piny and musty smell wafting over. He had a hot chocolate, with a blob of cream on top and chocolate sprinkles. He dipped a long finger into the cream and licked it.

'We must stop meeting like this,' he said.

'I've had enough,' I told him.

He reached across to half of my sandwich and took it. 'Waste not want not, as you people say,' he said.

I was stunned. I wanted to scream but I couldn't. I wanted to throw the tea in his face. He knew me inside out.

'I'll book a flight. I'll go over. I'm owed some time.'

Between mouthfuls of egg and bacon and soggy bread he said, 'Don't expect anything.' I could see the pulped sandwich in his mouth. He grinned. I had an urge to laugh but didn't give in to it.

Four

I got off the U-Bahn in the suburb of Mümmelmannsberg. A dump, even compared to parts of Gloucester. Lots of high-rises, graffiti, boarded windows, menace. North African youths with jeans halfway down their arses, thick gold chains, glaring at you, knowing you didn't belong in the area. A straggly blonde German girl with a vicious-looking scar across her cheek pushing a pram, eyes dead.

So he'd ended up here. Maybe I wouldn't have done any better. I'd only been to Hamburg once, just before I got out.

We'd done the Reeperbahn, the prozzies, a bit of hash, nothing serious. It wasn't my scene. I'd paid this half-caste girl just to talk. She kept laughing at everything I said for no reason I could see. I didn't tell Steve or Ammo that, of course.

She'd been surprised to hear from me, old Inga. And I was surprised she still lived where she did. She spent the first three minutes calling me all the names under the sun. I let her vent.

'I want to help if I can,' I said. She seemed to understand English much better than I remembered.

'You too late I think. Shit-useless bastard.'

'I've had a little windfall,' I told her. She didn't know what it meant.

'*Geld.* Money,' I clarified.

'You don't have to upset the boy. Just send the cheque here. It will be your first contribution. Congratulations.'

I heard a male voice in the background. Then the two of them whispering.

'Have you got a number for him?' I said.

'Forgotten his name?'

'David's number please?'

'I told you years ago. He is called Bernd. He doesn't need your middle name as a cast-off. He doesn't need his little English father at all.'

'Or you either, I suppose.'

'How much you giving him? He'll only spend it on that poison.'

I let the silence hang there. She gave me the mobile number and the address of where he was 'crashing' as she put it, and slammed the receiver down.

It took me four attempts to get any sense out of him. He didn't believe it was me. Well, how would he know one way or the other? He spoke English with an American twang. He had a younger voice than I'd imagined, a bit wispy, girly almost. I was shaking when I'd finished speaking to him, and my heart was going like the clappers. In the end he rang back and left a message when I was in the hotel shower. 8pm, Kandinskyallee 4-18. A pool club and bar called Gecko.

A group of youths, two Moroccan-looking, three probably German, appeared from nowhere, and one of them asked me for a light. I thought it could be a ruse. They had thick north-German accents. When they realised I wasn't German, as I was giving them use of my lighter, some of their act disappeared and they became almost friendly.

'You want some?' said the tall, heavy-set blond one in the black bomber jacket, and he mimed puffing on a cigarette. 'Or something different. Harder? Whatever you want. Good prices. A girl maybe. You like young ones?'

He slapped me on the back, a bit too hard. I was getting a bit nervy. 'I'm looking for the Gecko,' I told them.

Two of them sniggered, then a thin, pockmarked Moroccan spoke: 'Down to the end and right, past Aldi.' His English had a Black Country tinge. 'I lived in Wolverhampton for one year before coming here,' he told me, noting my surprise.

'We've got Aldi, too,' I told them.

They didn't look impressed.

Five

Inga had never sent me any pictures of the boy, so I wasn't sure what he'd look like. I wasn't sure if he ever had corrective surgery or how well it turned out. I sat on a high, uncomfortable metal stool at the gloomy bar, irritating Europop belting out over the clicking of pool balls and the shouts of jubilation or accusations of cheating from the half-a-dozen tables in front of me. Huge oblong posters of near-naked women, in acidic colours, nearly covered the walls

The Dortmunder beer tasted as I remembered. I had a little bowl of peanuts. At the bottom of the bowl I found a stubbed out fag. They didn't have the custom here of making little pencil marks on your beermat to show how many you'd had, so you could pay up at the end. It wasn't that sort of place. Mostly teenagers or early twenties, again a mix of North Africans, Germans, some Poles probably, and one choice looking Chinese bloke who kept staring at me. The barmaid looked at me oddly when I said I was waiting to meet Bernd.

'I'm not sure Bernd comes here anymore, but he used to all the time,' she said, in what I thought was a Bavarian dialect, on account of its singsongy nature. I impressed myself at how my understanding of the language was coming back, just by being around native speakers.

'We've made an arrangement to meet,' I told her, having to shout to get over the thudding bass and synthesised garbage from the speakers a few feet from my head.

The Chinese man, in a dark suit, which set him apart from the other punters, had got up when he heard the boy's name. He ambled over.

In his late thirties, wiry, something rat-like about him. He sort of sized me up. My fist automatically balled up. 'I don't think you are in the right place,' he said, sneering at me. 'Maybe down the street. Der Ficken Club, ja?' He looked away, pointed at a bottle behind the bar, and the barmaid promptly filled a shot glass.

He wanted me out. The club he mentioned was a way of telling me to fuck off. Ficken being the operative word.

The street door opened and a young man came in, along with a gust of cold wind. Skinny build, pale brown hair, dodgy moustache, long black leather coat over a white jumper and jeans. He looked nervously around the place in quick jerky movements of his head. I didn't get direct eye contact. He sat at the other end of the bar, ordered a beer. Hunched over, his hand over the side of his face like he didn't want to draw any attention. Something told me it was him. The Chinese man had wandered back to his little round surveying table. My heart was going again and my mouth was dry so I took a long drink, then dropped my fag in the dregs. It hissed.

Some of the pool-playing youths were giving each other meaningful looks. The music was turned up a notch. The rasping female voice kept shouting 'Do it, do it, do it, do it to me', over and over again. One of the North Africans nodded at the Chinese man.

I got off the stool and started walking to the young man who had never called me Dad. Just then, three of them rushed past me, two North Africans reaching into their jackets, and one shaven-headed white who had something in his hand. They covered him from my view. I saw a flurry of blows and slashing movements. It was a strangely quiet act under that pulsating noise, like a silent movie or something happening under water. I didn't move closer till they had all pelted out of the exit, one of them dropping something metallic on the beer-sticky floor.

He lay slumped against the wall, and I stood over him. His white jumper now had these spreading red patches. His face and neck were slashed. Something had gone through his eye. It was a raw dark red hole. He was still breathing. Beneath the moustache I could make out the wavy scar line. They'd done a terrific job. I didn't see me in his face, or her. But I saw my own father. The hair and jaw-line, the high cheekbones.

I spun around. The Chinese man's table was empty. Just his shot glass stood there. Others were leaving the bar in a great hurry. I caught one by the sleeve. He wrenched it away.

'Turn that fucking shit off,' I shouted. 'He's dying. He's dying. Call an ambulance someone, for fuck's sake.' They all ignored me, pushing through the exit in knots of two and three till the place was empty except for the barmaid.

I rushed behind the bar and ripped the lead out of the back of the CD player. Instant quiet. And that shocked me more than anything. 'Where's the phone?' I shouted at her. Mine had chosen just the right moment to die.

She stared at me like I was a loony. 'That's Bernd, isn't it, you stupid bitch? That's Bernd on the floor there, and you know it.'

'I… I don't know him. He's never come in here before. I don't know why this has happened.' Tears were welling in her big stupid blue eyes.

I got through and waited for them to come. I walked over to

him to put my rolled up jacket under his head. I felt his hand. It was very cold. Blood came away on my shirt. I touched it like they do in films.

'You achieved something.' It came from behind me.

It was my old mucker, my tracker, my reliable ghost, my little voice of sanity. He was lining up to pot a black. The light from the green-glassed overhead unit bleached out his features, sharpening the contrast of his dark beard against his skin. He still wore that daft hat.

'What did I?' I said.

'He did not die alone.'

I got down and cradled Bernd's gashed head in my lap. I stroked his hair. I covered his damaged eye with my palm. His jumper front now had an even coating of red.

The barmaid had gone to some upper room in the building. I could hear voices above me. Maybe the Chinese man was up there.

I heard a sharp click of cue on ball and the satisfying thwock as the black went down. I looked up. The cue lay across the table. But for now I needed to keep stroking that soft young hair. I had to keep faith with that breathless body.

Restoration

Sarah Bower

The day I returned to work was the first real spring day of
that year. The plane trees along St. Martins' Place were in bud,
squadrons of miniature pale yellow blimps against a postcard
blue sky. Sunlight glinted off bus windows and cyclists' goggles and the dust on the pavements had a sheen to it, like finely
ground coal. My fellow commuters wore pallid smiles and
squinted, mole-like, in the unaccustomed brightness. Perhaps
it was my mood, but I couldn't help feeling Londoners looked
more at home in grey weather than on days like this.

I wasn't ready to come back, but nor could I stay cooped up
in the flat any longer. The last time Sabrina came round, that
was what she said. She dumped the supermarket bags on the
kitchen counter, put the kettle on and said,

'This has to stop, Cat. All you're doing is making it worse.'

When you grieve, your mind seems to fragment. The part
of mine that remained rational knew she was right. I had been
lying on the sofa for so long I tended to feel dizzy when I
stood up and my legs felt like Bambi's, and I had no idea when
I had last washed, or eaten, or slept, or woken up. The other

parts, though, the parts lodged inside me like shattered glass, were all screaming no, I couldn't possibly go out. What if you came back? What if you climbed the two flights of stairs, running your hand along the wrought iron banister rail as you always did, until it encountered the lumpy flaw in the paintwork at the turn of the second landing? What if you lifted your hand then, as you always did, as though it had been burned, fished your key from your pocket, unlocked the door and entered the narrow hallway redolent of old books, and stood there, your words of reconciliation lined up on your lovely, clever tongue, and I wasn't there to hear them? I had to stay here, on the sofa, my head at just the right angle to take in the missing-tooth gap left by your Roberto Bolano novels and the rim of dust marking the space where your iPod dock stood.

'You should take a shower then call Edmund and tell him you're coming back on Monday,' said Sabrina, placing a cup of white tea in front of me. I was fond of Sabrina and wanted to believe she was right and so, that Monday, the first day of spring, I found myself walking briskly towards the gallery from Charing Cross tube and not one of my fellow, sun-dazzled commuters could have known how I felt as the spaces left by your books, your toothbrush, your body in the bed, were ripped slowly from my skin like lengths of duct tape.

Edmund, a kindly caricature of an art historian in his yellow waistcoat and flamboyant bow tie, had arranged a 'little outing' for me, to keep me, as he saw it, from pining in the basement workshop that was my regular haunt.

'And the weather,' he said, flapping a plump hand at the tall sash window behind him. 'A jaunt out to Lambeth in this will be just perfect. I quite wish I was coming with you.' He wasn't because it was a routine job, to photograph a portrait of Archbishop William Warham for a schools information pack on the Tudors. I would be accompanied by Sabrina, who usually worked with me, recording the various stages in the restorations I undertook.

The Archbishop's portrait was in a small, rather dark sitting room at the back of the palace, a room whose air of being overlooked chimed with the elegiac in my own mood, which wound about the shards of pain like a mist. As I flexed my fingers into cotton gloves, ready to lift the painting off the wall and carry it to a table beneath the single window where Sabrina had set up her equipment, my eye was caught by another portrait, as neglected as the room itself, the paint cracked and grimy. While Sabrina photographed Archbishop Warham, I wandered across to look at it. A brass legend pinned to the frame informed me it was a representation of Katherine Parr.

'Sabrina… come over here a minute.' My voice, that had been used for little but sobbing and keening in the past three weeks, two days and – I glanced at my watch at this point – five hours since you left, sounded querulous and alien to me. Yet I felt, for the first time since that morning, a tiny shift inside me, an uncurling, as if a clenched fist had begun to relax.

'What have you seen?' Sabrina's voice, as she peered over my shoulder, echoed my own suppressed excitement.

'I don't think this is Katherine Parr. I don't think it can be. Look at the headdress, the neckline…' My gloved finger traced a line in the air from the peak of the jewelled kennel headdress to the square neckline trimmed with gold tape. I noted the delicacy with which the artist had shaded the rise of his subject's cleavage above her corseted bodice. And remembered your tongue, tracing a fine saliva trail between my breasts. 'And the frame,' I ploughed on. 'All too early for Parr. She'd have been a little girl when this was painted. I think this is…'

'Catherine of Aragon.' Sabrina squeezed my shoulder. She had been there when we met. She knew it was Catherine of Aragon who had brought us together.

'The Queen Catherine,' you had pronounced, gazing up at the pub sign. 'Now there's a catch-all.' I knew you were drunk; your team had been sitting at the next table to ours during the quiz, and all four of you were quite loud, not regulars, not focused, as we were, on the jovial bitterness of our long-standing rivalries. 'Braganza, Valois, Howard…'

'Aragon,' I interrupted, and was about to explain how you could tell from the portrait bust adorning the pub sign when Sabrina dragged me away. I wouldn't have said anything if you hadn't begun your list with two Catherines who were not queens of Henry VIII. That showed some originality. The following week, although you didn't attend the quiz night, I discovered you'd left a note for me behind the bar. Addressed to *the blonde woman in the red mac.*

How do you know? the note said. And a phone number. That was all. Abrupt to the point of rudeness, yet it was the right question. You always asked the right questions, but I fell into the habit of giving the wrong answers.

'Catherine of Aragon,' I repeated, feeling the sting of yet more tears in my sandpapered eyes.

'We're not here for this one, though, are we?' Sabrina insisted.

'No, but…'

'No buts.'

'If it's wrongly attributed we have a responsibility…' I peered more closely at the portrait, 'and I'm sure… look.' I pointed to a fine line around the throat, just above the shortest of the subject's three strings of large pearls.

Sabrina laughed. 'If it was Catherine Howard I'd suggest the executioner had drawn that on.'

I wanted to tell her I thought the line indicated a change of hand, perhaps some tampering with the features of the face, but found I couldn't speak. There was something ineffably moving about the line, fine, but clear, no effort made to disguise it, and above it the coarsely worked, homogeneous features that made such a jarring contrast with the details of the gown, and jewels, and the subtly outlined breasts. That the once loved should be effaced with such brutality, such carelessness.

I waited in a blur of small distractions while Edmund negotiated with Lambeth Palace. He wouldn't have bothered – I could tell from the quizzical look he gave me when I burst into

his office with my half articulate account of our discovery –
except for the circumstances. So I made sure not to express
my impatience, to try to await the outcome of the negotiations
with grace.

By the time the painting was delivered to my basement
studio, the plane trees were in full leaf, their palmate foliage
splintering sunlight into glitter as I walked beneath them, or
smacked and cowed by the rain that seemed to storm in every
afternoon in a tropical pattern that made my skin crawl with
unease. I arrived one morning and found it there, propped
against the wall. I was disconcerted by the lack of ceremony
attending its arrival. I couldn't see it as Edmund and Sabrina
and the others must see it, as an insignificant and undemand-
ing project designed to coax me back from the edge of the
crevasse that had opened up in my heart.

There was a note from Edmund, on a yellow post-it stuck to
the workbench in front of the painting.

*Do you think it might be a match for the 1513 Henry? Some similari-
ties in the framing?*

Edmund was showing me the way I might go. If I could
match up this painting with the 1513 Henry, then we would
have a story, a reason to hang my Catherine rather than consign
her to the stacks on the floor below mine, to a dehumidified
steel cabinet, rat proof, bomb proof, light proof. Life proof.
Make her a match, he was saying, give her a reason to exist.
Though he meant it kindly, I was angry that Catherine's entitle-
ment should still depend on her husband, and then wondered
if my anger was what Edmund had hoped for.

'You should be livid,' Sabrina said when you left. 'I am.' But
grief is all consuming. It must be assiduously tended, like a
reluctant fire you cannot leave to go out because it is all that
stands between you and the cold and the night. Grief leaves
you no energy for anything you might want for yourself, like
anger, or self-esteem, or good memories.

Instead of throwing Edmund's note away I folded it into the
marsupial pocket of my apron, where it crunched softly as I

rolled up my sleeves and sat down to work.

Do you remember me telling you an oil painting can be cleaned with human saliva? We were kissing in the kitchen, eggs for a Spanish omelette half whipped, the edge of the counter digging into the base of my spine, and when we parted, you saying you must open the wine so it could breathe before dinner, fine, silver strings of saliva kept us fleetingly conjoined. That was when I told you. A cotton bud moistened with spit. You looked, I think now, with hindsight, disconcerted.

In our workshops we don't use saliva, of course. We use exquisitely balanced emulsions and neutralisers and varnish removers, and despite the provision of extractor fans and the wearing of goggles, the fumes are enough to desiccate the tear ducts. Once I had begun work on Catherine I no longer cried. I sat alone on the sofa and stared at your empty chair, and wished I had a television so I could watch soap operas in which the partings of lovers were consolingly habitual. I drank whisky until I was anaesthetized against the thought of the half empty bed, lurking in the shadows like some mythological monster. My sleep was of the fitful, feverish kind from which you awake more exhausted than when you fell into it. But I did not cry.

And I worked assiduously to excavate the features of the young Catherine of Aragon from beneath the disguise foisted on her, no doubt, by crass political expediency and cowardice. Some evenings I would be made aware of the day's passing only when the caretaker popped his head around my door to say he was locking up, and to remember to reset the alarm when I let myself out. On others, Edmund would bring my working day to an end by appearing in the studio with a bottle of single malt and two glasses, and feign an interest in my poor queen whose reputation for stubborn loyalty has made her so much duller to posterity than the glamorous Howard girls or fey Seymour. Even phlegmatic Cleves and stalwart Parr have had a better press than my Catherine.

'She was lovely, you know,' I told Edmund on one of these

occasions, 'until love wrecked her.' Poor Edmund coughed and topped up my glass, and his well-shaven jowls turned a deeper shade of damson.

In the end I proved it to him. The morning I knocked on his office door to tell him I believed Catherine was ready for the scrutiny of the hanging committee she was, I believe, as lovely as she must have been on her wedding day. Her grey eyes appraised us with cool intelligence but her full lower lip, with its suggestive cleft, spoke of a hotter, deeper wisdom not learned from books but arrived in her fully formed and half tamed and scarcely understood. No trace remained of the coarse, embittered features of the imposter Sabrina I had rumbled at Lambeth Palace.

I waited alone in my studio for the committee's decision. Sabrina came in with coffees from the café across the road, but quickly understood I couldn't speak to her. I was locked into the blank tension of waiting. I felt sick and light-headed. My bowels griped. With the extractors switched off, the studio was pervaded by a dusty, ticking silence. I stared at my phone, lying on the swept workbench, and thought of you, of waiting for your texts (you never liked talking on the phone). I imagined you now as a djinn trapped inside the phone and myself the one foolish enough to be charmed by your pleas for liberation. When the phone rang, I nearly jumped out of my skin.

'They send their congratulations,' said Edmund. 'We'll hang it with the 1513 Henry. Awfully well done, Cat. Welcome back.'

My Catherine was hung at seven in the morning, the autumn dawn just beginning to spread itself behind the skyline of the Square Mile whose towers rose into the luminous sky like relics of a drowned world. You had been gone for six months. I had stopped counting the days. I had changed my hair, and rearranged the books on the shelves to conceal the gaps left by yours. I had given our bed linen to the charity shop on the corner next to the butchers' and turned the mattress so the imprint of your body was now lost among the bedsprings. Everyone said I was getting better.

Regardless of the early hour, we drank champagne, Edmund, Sabrina, Charlie and Dean, in pristine overalls and white gloves, who had lifted Catherine into position on her husband's right hand, and I. I toasted Catherine. Edmund toasted me, then gathered us all with an expansive gesture of his arms and summoned us to breakfast in his office.

'Almond croissants,' he said, round-eyed as a schoolboy delving in a tuck box, 'and monkey oolong.'

'Delish,' said Sabrina.

'Give me a minute,' I asked, and he shepherded the rest away. Conservators develop intimate relationships with the pieces they work on, everyone in the gallery understands this and allowances are made.

I gazed at Catherine across five hundred years, across a few feet of ash plank floor, pooling pale gold under the halogen downlighters. I looked at Henry, half turned towards her, though his regard, wary and shrewd, was angled out at the gallery. Catherine, by contrast, gazed straight back at me, and I thought of your lower lip, and how I used to love to graze it with my teeth and how you murmured, smiling, that you weren't sure about biting but thought you might get used to it. I suppose you didn't.

I reached into my bag for my door key, not the one I usually carried but yours, the one you discarded on the claret table in the hall when you left. It was attached to a Gucci key ring, for which you had apologised, once, saying it had been a gift from your brother, whose tastes were different from yours. Advancing on Henry with the key in my outstretched hand I gouged a long tear in the canvas, from top right to bottom left. The throaty ripping of old canvas sounded loud in the empty gallery. The rent passed through his velvet cap, through one puffy eye, through his patrician, aquiline nose. It tore his fur collar and one satin sleeve. It missed his prim, pursed mouth completely.

That was a mistake. Stepping up to the painting, across the

white line on the floor that marks the invisible boundary between the portraits and their public, I dug my fingers into the gash and tore it wider, obliterating the bottom half of Henry's face. His remaining eye, the cheek beneath it torn away, put me in mind of a pig in an abattoir. I lifted him off the wall and dumped him face down on the floor. I tossed your key after him.

79 Green Gables

John D Rutter

It had only taken us a couple of hours round the M25 and up the M11 to get back to Green Gables. The village was the same as always, pink pansies in hanging baskets dangling from leaning Tudor houses; funny how the baskets up North never seem to thrive like that. The incline of ancient walls washed with pastel shades of terracotta and blue seemed to be perfectly designed to fit between the handsome oaks and mature sycamores.

I'd always loved the crunching sound as I pulled onto the gravel drive and I'd learnt the knack of lifting the wrought iron gates simultaneously so the bolts slotted into their holes. I wondered how many more times I'd do that.

Pippa was quickly out of the car, leaving me to sort everything out as usual. She hugged her mum while I unloaded our matching suitcases, which meant lifting out the camping gear. I scratched her case, the larger one, on the exhaust, leaving a long black scar.

Her father Henry came to help and offered a formal handshake while we exchanged awkward greetings. 'Good trip?' he asked, prompting me to describe the traffic all the way from Calais. Pippa and her mum disappeared into the kitchen, nattering away. *Would she tell her?* Thankfully Digger was home from Iraq and it was too early for him to have started drinking.

'Ah, the prodigal brother-in-law returns,' he grinned, pulling me into a bear hug. His father gave a disapproving look at his youngest child's affected cockney slur.

'You buying me a pint after dinner then?' I asked.

'I should coco, Bruv!'

At least there was that to look forward to. Digger could be a bit of an idiot, but his permanent smirk was exactly what I needed in the circumstances, and I'd told him what was going on before we went. We'd probably be having fish for dinner, it being a Friday, and summer pudding because her mum had got it into her head that it was my favourite. She hugged me as I went into the warm kitchen. The AGA was on as always; I had to loosen my collar.

'You've certainly caught the sun!' she said. Pippa didn't join in; she hadn't mentioned my tan once. Her mind must have been somewhere else. She was busying herself with the dog.

'Yes, the weather was fantastic. What's it been like here?'

'We had a spot of rain on Tuesday, but otherwise we've had a bit of an Indian summer. I've made your favourite, summer pudding.'

I looked for a knowing smile from Pippa. She didn't look up from the dog until Norbert scuttled across the tiles to greet me himself, wetting my hand and my leg.

'You must tell us *all* about it,' her mum said.

I wandered back to the car to get the AA road atlas of France onto which I had marked our route. I could kill the half hour before dinner, eat, then escape to the pub. The atlas was in the pocket behind the passenger seat. I felt my diary as I stretched round to reach it. I held it for a moment, then shoved it deep into the pocket.

Henry peered at the map over his glasses as I described our trip through Normandy and down the West coast of France.

'Oh, yes, I remember Honfleur, pretty little harbour,' he said. 'What year was that, Bunny?'

I'd never quite dared to call my mother-in-law Bunny. Her blue eyes widened. She smiled, 'It was when the boys were still pre-school, Pippa must have been about five.'

So, it's not just me that'll remember Honfleur for the rest of my life. I've images etched in my mind of a merry-go-round and the fishing boats and the plats de fruit de mer we shared, best seafood I'd ever had, and the delicate white wine, Guillac, and the full-moon and a thousand stars. And I remember Pippa refusing to kiss me.

'Let's not spoil this,' she said when I moved towards her.

'John, help Henry set the table will you?' Bunny said. 'You're in your usual place. And Pippa, go and see if you can find that brother of yours.'

'Where's the other one?' I asked.

'Luke? He's off at some rave tonight; cramming it all in before he sets off for Antarctica.'

I can't imagine what that isolation must feel like, though I suppose I'd had some pretty lonely moments in the car these last two weeks.

Henry had already laid out the silver cutlery. I hadn't paid much attention when he told me the history of the dining table every Christmas. It was one of those Louis - Quatorze or Quinze. I did know that a red wine stain would be like crashing a car or killing the dog.

'Why don't you be in charge of the wine?' said Henry nodding at a bottle of Chardonnay. He was always friendly to me but he couldn't help but sound like a senior officer when he asked you to do something.

'We've brought back a case of Saint-Émilion, last year's.'

'Marvellous, one can't beat a good claret.'

Soon we were chomping our way through Bunny's fish pie, Digger and me taking turns to top up each other's wine glasses. She can drive tomorrow, I thought. It's her turn and I'm not going to get through this night sober.

I was forced to eat a huge portion of summer pudding which was too tangy and fought with the wine. I picked at the cheese while Pippa recounted how the farmer / restaurateur at Quimper drew the menu on the table cloth and how, when I'd pointed at the cow he'd drawn she'd rattled off a few sentences in French and he came back with a Chateaubriand that had not been cooked at all. Bleu they call it; my word's raw. She told them about the campsites and the night I cut my finger and we both had uncontrollable fits of laughter at the enormous bandage she applied. But she didn't mention the diary.

I'd decided to write a diary for the first time in my 29 years to help me deal with the situation. I'd crammed my thoughts between the lines of last year's McAlpine Construction pocket diary with an IKEA pencil. I'd written everything from the music on the radio to my conflicting emotions as we drove through the endless French countryside. On the last night we sat by the riverbank behind our tent with a plastic jug of Medoc and she persuaded me to let her read it. By the second glass I caved; she could still get her way. I quoted a line from a Del Amitri song, 'Sometimes I could sell my soul just to sit and watch you smoke.' She sighed and opened the diary. When she'd finished about an hour later, she closed it, handed it back and lit up.

'So, what do you think?'

'It's very well written.'

We didn't make eye contact during dinner except once when I caught her glance as I poured a large glass of port and topped up Digger's, breaching the anti-clockwise rule. She rolled her eyes at me, so I turned to the antique dresser and the two orange-brown Kutani vases I'd always liked. I had the oddest thought; they'd have ended up with us eventually when the oldies (as she called them) died. That wasn't going to happen now.

Half a bottle of wine and the port guided me safely through dinner and Digger was tugging my sleeve before the formalities of clearing up started. I half-heartedly offered to do the washing up; Henry began to say what a good egg that would

make me until Bunny explained things to him with her eyes
and Digger and I were off into the village.

I took a cigarette off him before we reached the gate.

'Well, if you ask me, I think she's being a silly bitch. Have
you decided what's gonna 'appen?' he said.

'Dunno, Our Kid. She says she needs a bit of time to decide,
but I think it's too late. Look, can we talk about something
else? I just fancy getting pissed and having a game of cards. I'll
deal with all that when we get home.'

'Well, you know you can always call me don't you, mate?'

'I know, but I think the way it works is you keep your own
books and relatives. She'll probably bring *him* next year.'

'Fack off!'

He pushed the pub door open and the familiar murmur
blanketed me. Before I reached the bar he'd already shaken
hands with several of his friends. We'd be here until closing
time then cards back at the house. I could gamble away my last
holiday cash.

By the time I'd blown £20 at three card brag my head was hurting and the top half of the lounge was full of dense smoke. I
made my excuses and Digger beamed while he dealt.

'Remember what I said.' Then he did that phone thing with his
left hand. I nodded, but we both knew.

I sneaked into Pippa's room and crawled in silently beside
her. I thought of the first time we sneaked around at night
here; one of the buttons came off her blouse and we bumped
heads looking for it and both got the giggles.

I lay at the outer edge of the bed on my back. She rolled over
to the far side without speaking. I was exhausted after the journey and three pints of Adnams on top of the wine were enough
to send me into a deep sleep for the first time in two weeks.

When I woke the sun was yelling through the window and my
mouth tasted of tar and cheese. Pippa was nowhere in sight. I
said good morning to her parents as I poured myself a strong
mug of coffee. Digger was always louder and later than me so

I never felt the need to apologise for an occasional big drink. Besides, it didn't really matter anymore.

I held my coffee in both hands as I stepped out into the garden. My normal pattern was to stroll the 100 yards to the great old oak tree at the bottom where the horses would come and greet me and then I'd stride back up to the house. Today I sat on Uncle Oliver's bench facing the kitchen with the sun on my back. The bench matched the one he'd made for our wedding present. Would she take that too?

Norbert scampered up to me with his rubber ring. They seem to be especially stupid hounds, Bassets, but at least if you ignored him the first time he understood that you didn't want to play. I didn't used to like dogs.

'Alright, daft dog, one throw. I'll be gone soon.'

Bunny shuffled out of the kitchen, a bit hesitant. She had such a lovely smile, I doubt Pippa will look that good at 57.

'It's going to be a lovely day, shame you have to go so soon.'

'Better get off early, beat Birmingham before lunchtime.'

She sat next to me and Norbert followed her. We had one of those pregnant pauses. I didn't know what to say so I waited for her to break first.

'You know you'll always be welcome here, don't you?'

Somehow that went straight to the back of my eyes and I had to clear my throat before I could reply. She'd talked to Pippa. I put my hand on hers; her skin was so soft, exactly like Grandma's when I was small.

'I will miss you all, even daft dog…'

'Oh, you don't need to feel…' she saw my head shake.

'This will be the last time I ever come here.' I looked away out of embarrassment and when I turned back two tears were having a race down her cheeks.

Pippa appeared and the moment was gone. I stood, took a last look at the garden and headed straight through the house to where our bags were standing to attention by the front door. I lifted one case in each hand and left the house.

By the time I had reorganised the car boot everyone had

come out apart from Digger who was still sleeping off his drink. Henry firmly shook my hand and I got in the car. Pippa squeezed her mum. Henry grabbed Norbert so he didn't run in front of the car when Pippa reversed out too fast. I wound down the window as the gate clanged shut.

'Say bye to the boys for me, won't you?'

They looked at each other. Bunny smiled and waved. Then Pippa drove us away.

Death and the Maiden

Maggie Ling

Watching him had become a comforting pastime, a part of her life. Something she did when washing the dishes; she seldom used the dishwasher now. He was someone to look down on while she hand-washed her 'delicates' – previously tossed into the washing machine without a thought. These so-called delicates even extending to barely worn sweaters and shirts, all clearly labelled Machine Washable, yet all lovingly immersed in soapy bubbles in the kitchen sink.

She had not gone out of her way to observe him. No. She was just going about her daily routine. It was *he* who had placed himself in her line of vision. He, two floors below, who had given her – looking down from her top-floor casement on the other side of the square – an 'opened-curtained' view on his life.

And the most comforting thing of all was: he was always alone. Had been alone for weeks. Or was it months? Yes. He had been alone since early November. Though he had gone away for Christmas. Home, she supposed. Wherever that might be? This had saddened her at first. But then late Boxing Day afternoon she had seen slits of light filtering through the Venetian blind, and come the morning there he was, back at his desk again. She even found herself able to enjoy a film that afternoon, curling up on the sofa, quite relaxed, halfway through going to the kitchen for refreshments, looking down, seeing him, still sitting there. Had he, she wondered, moved his desk to that position purely out of consideration for her?

She had not seen him move it. It had been there when she returned from work: two weeks after he had moved in.

She had gone to the sink to fill the kettle, expecting to see only the glow of a hall light leeching through a half-open door, to be met by the sight of him, sitting at his computer, a desk lamp warmly highlighting his face. And instead of putting a tea bag in a mug, as she might have done, as she had always done, found herself searching for an unopened packet of loose Darjeeling she thought she still had, and set the tea to brew in her large, largely unused, teapot, pulling out a stool to drink it, there in the kitchen.

It was at breakfast time the following morning that she noticed a large filing cabinet had replaced the exercise bike, previously visible in the corner of the room. So he would no longer expose his half naked torso to her gaze, no longer lie there, stretching, lifting weights, doing energetic push ups before, half disappearing behind the half-drawn curtains, she would see his feet peddling to nowhere on the bike.

Now he barely disappeared from view: the blind was always up and he, more often than not, was always there. Though not there in the mornings: not before she went to work. And seldom there on Saturday mornings. But almost always on Sundays – another considerate move on his part. Sundays were always difficult. Although, she'd felt quite slovenly, shuffling into the kitchen, seeing him there. She had made a New Year's Resolution: vowed never again to spend most of Sunday in her dressing gown, next day going out to buy three pairs of pull-on lounging trousers with matching tops in the sale.

*

I've seen her up there, up at that window, looking down. Saw her soon after I moved in here: those first few days when I used this room as my exercise space. I know the park's only ten minutes up the road, but at the beginning of something I barely go out. Like to keep my head down, keep concentrated – even when there's nothing much to concentrate on. 'For fuck's sake!' my wife used to say, 'How the hell can you write about life if you never live it?' I remember once countering this much-used insult by quoting a much-quoted bit of Socratic wisdom: 'Well,' I said, with all the irony I could muster, 'The Unexamined Life and all that . . .' 'Words! Words! Words!' she said, slamming the door.

I *had* put my desk under the window in the living room. But this block being right on the T-junction, I found looking out on the wide, busy street, leading straight north to the park, quite distracting. Especially since, even in early November, the Christmas lights were already twink-twinkling from dawn to bloody dusk. No way was I ready for such jollity. Not this year. Sorry. Not *last* year. Is it really already mid January? How is it that Time can drag, yet, at the same time, speed by in a flash?

Anyway, as soon as I'd ripped out those dreary curtains, put up a cheap blind (which, since the room's too dark when it's down, I needn't have bothered buying) and dragged the desk here, under the window, I felt the slightest tug-tugging of something: an upturned thought, bordering on a vague idea, beginning to surface in the dishevelled bunch of nervous ganglia that constitutes my brain; felt this the right space to be in – work-wise.

There's something sombre, something punitive, about sitting here, looking out from this tall sash window – Georgian, in itself quite elegant – into the dingy 'funnel' of buildings out there, all looking in on themselves. Such a contrast to the living room. The other side of the block all glittering lights, all spend, spend, spend neon, while this side smacks of Grub Street. Or worse! Don't know if anyone really uses that dark square, four floors down. Occasionally an echoing cough splutters up to me. Every once in a while I hear what sounds like a rubbish bin – the old-fashioned, galvanised sort – being scraped across the ground, hear the shuffle of feet, picture a chained-together ring of prisoners circling the square, imagine an animated Dorè etching, straight out of Newgate, going on down there.

Becky used to tell me I was *chained* to my desk. Ironic really. Though I didn't think I was then, I most certainly am now. Thanks a bunch, Becky.

I thought she might stop looking down at me – the woman on the top floor, not Becky; don't think Becky'll ever stop looking down on me. Thought the woman up there might be a bit of a middle-aged perv: one who, for some unfathomable reason, got off on my OK torso. Figured when she saw me tap-tapping away down here – or, most likely, *not* tap-tapping away – she might stop looking. I mean that woman spends half her life in her kitchen. Surely there's more to her flat than that one room? I can just about make her out – the woman up there, not my wife. Thought I'd made Becky out a long time ago. My mistake.

Some might think it a good thing: feeling you have some understanding of another human being, believing they have some understanding of you, and finding a degree of contentment in that. I imagined Becky and me to be in that mythical place. But, truth is, my wife, for all she says now, was never really into contentment. No. Becky has some mistaken notion about women and mystery. Has a need to hold on to it, hold a part of herself back, in some misbegotten, misguided, *mysterious* way.

I think I've seen her, the woman up there, seen her in the street a couple of times. I'm pretty certain it was her. Anyway, if it was, she's a brown sort of woman: brown hair, brown coat, brown boots – brownish skin, even. Not brown-skinned. Not Afro-Caribbean or anything. Just a tad muddy. Swarthy, you could say – except, you can't say that now without it sounding like an insult. Her skin has the 'lived-in' quality of someone not overly concerned with her appearance. Not *not* concerned, you understand, not one stage off a cardboard box and a street corner, just someone unbothered by such things. And, perhaps, since we're here in the heart of the city, where a complete makeover is the bat of a false eyelash away, a woman not too flush with money. Maybe, right now, she and I have that much in common.

This woman – the woman I *think* is this woman – looked a couple of decades older than me. Although I suspect she might look a bit older than she is. She's not tall, but not tiny, and has a kind, if slightly tense, face. The kind of woman who looks a little out of place in this part of town. Looks of another age. One in which Being had more clout than Looking – in the sense of looking good, of caring how one is perceived. Looks the sort who would be more at home in the country, where she might dissolve into the monochrome, clod-brown winter fields.

*

I was born in a field in October 1959 – or so my mother told me, six years later. I can still remember her telling me the story of my birth. Except, after she told me, I somehow reconfigured her words, and for some time, beyond a time when I should have known better, remembered it this way, *You were born of a field*, imagining my childhood self emerging from Mother Earth, pushing through her fertile surface like a plump, ripe seed, bursting into life.

I had chalked up almost a decade on Mother Earth before my schoolteacher sought to correct me on this fundamental principal of life. 'Heaven's, child! Did your mother not tell you how you arrived in the world?' I pretended my mother had not told me. This re-telling of my life story coming as a sudden disappointment to me. Now I was like everyone else. I had come into the world, not free, not self-determined, not in control of my arrival, but tied, chained by flesh and blood to another flesh and blood human being, to my *own* flesh and blood, to my mother.

My father was not present at my birth. Though only two fields away at the time, turning the last of that season's stubble, the thrum-thrum-thrumming of the tractor and caw-caw-cawing of seagulls circling overhead, was quite enough to drown out my mother's hopeless cries.

More than an hour had gone by before, in need of his long overdue refreshment, making his way back to the house, my father came upon his wife and newly born child – his only child – tied together as one in the damp meadow grass, his flask of tea and trencherman's supply of sandwiches fallen to the ground beside them.

Sometimes I think I, too, can remember that day, can call up from deep within my unknowing, floating self, the slimy pond creature who slithered onto the grass that day, squirming on the end of the umbilical cord, unable to break free. For, even now, when I think of it, I see white clouds scudding above my head, feel my heart racing, as a baby's heart races, with joy, or with fear; think of this first sight of the world and wish I could see it again, could begin again.

*

Thing is, the Brown Woman is beginning to bugger up my plotline.

'Yeah,' my editor says, skimming over the synopsis. 'It'll do fine, Grant. But you'd better crack on. *Fast!* You know we're planning to catch the Christmas market next year. We'll just have to rush this one through. Still, you're such a pro. You've managed a book in six months before now… So?' Duncan gives me one of his raised eyebrow looks.

So? I nearly say, Write the damn thing yourself then. Because, y'know what, Duncan, I've had enough of pleasing you, pleasing my agent, pleasing my publicist – even pleasing my readers. Had enough of being a book factory: churning them out just because I can, because they sell – just about. Just because my name's embossed on the moody, monochrome covers; just because I'm 'Kindled', am beloved of supermarkets – as well as a few kindly independent bookshops owners; because I sell at three-for-two, as well as, every once in a while, precisely the price I *should* sell at. Because of this everyone's happy. Everyone except me. But hey! Who cares? I'm just the writer. And, irony of ironies, this time, even *Becky's* happy.

My estranged wife dared to call me the other evening, 'How's it going?' she dares to ask in her soft, caring voice. 'Fine,' I say. 'Don't worry. The mortgage'll be paid. I won't renege on promises made. Just as long as you don't call me. Email, if you must. Otherwise, the cheque'll be in the post, as and when – or, rather, in your brand new bank account.'

Having finally got myself a plotline, as crap as that plotline may be, I, quite literally, cannot afford to waste time on this one. We're nine months behind schedule, you see. Interesting, that time frame.

*

My mother never sought to inform me of the physical processes involved in my growing from child to adult. Which may partially explain why I have never quite made it in the world of adults. Why, after all these years in the city, I still feel apart from them, feel more connected to the earth than to its people. But at least you can get lost in a city, can melt away, lose the past – or try to lose it.

As a child, I remember observing traces of blood in the toilet bowl. Thinking my mother had contracted some internal, terminal affliction, I waited, fearing for her life, but saying nothing. Nothing happened. In fact my mother blossomed. Again I said nothing, never expressing my fears, or my relief – if that emotion was felt. Our relationship, you see, was not one enamoured of intimacies. She and I dealt with the very basics of life. The everyday acts of eating and sleeping, the only subjects worthy of our daily discourse, her daily cross-examination; the same dialogue tossed back and forth, without thought. *What* I thought mattered little to her. What went on beneath her daughter's cranium could remain a mystery, as far as she was concerned.

Menstruation – our common *curse* – was something else my mother chose not to share with me. I was fourteen years and eight months old when I had my first period, and fifteen years and nine months when I had my first child. Both events were washed away in a similar fashion.

*

Does that woman have no friends? Hey! Who's talking? Is it the work? Or is it me? Or has Becky been ratchettng up the anti? Whatever it is, most of the time it *is* just me, this room, this computer, and a stream of emails – plus the odd harassing call from Duncan. And, as nice as it is to have *someone* call me, Duncan is not someone I need right now.

I should call, text around, send a few emails, say: Listen, folks! It's not how it looks. I have *not* walked out on my butter-wouldn't-melt-in-her-mouth pregnant wife. Why would I want to do that? It's *she* who has walked out on me. It's just, she's done it by staying put. Well, what else could I do? Though I might've got a bit more empathy if I'd reassembled a couple of those cardboard boxes I'd been dutifully flattening, handed them to Becky and booted her straight out the door.

'Grant . . ?' she says, in her sweet, girly questioning tone, 'Are you busy right now?'

'Hmm?' I say, looking down at a flattened box, thinking: What Einstein of the cardboard universe works out how to cut this stuff in such a way that it assembles and dismantles like this? Makes writing a damn detective story look like child's play. Then, tuning in to what Becky is saying, I hear the word *baby*, hear myself saying, 'When? *When* did you say this baby's due?'

And that's when it falls apart again: this marriage I thought we'd reassembled.

I expect sob stories have been doing the rounds. Hell! Who wouldn't believe them? Me here in my bachelor pad, pretending to work. Beautiful blonde Becky, at home, carrying the baby. Well if Becky's so good at sob stories, maybe she should write her own misery memoir. Since most of them are bags of hogwash, she'd be in good company. Could clean up. I could take time out. Retrain. Be that engineer my mother always wanted me to be. Or, better still, write a book that doesn't have a cool dude detective at its heart.

She's still up there, the Brown Woman, doing her slow motion washing up. How many dishes can one woman use? Unless there's a wild dinner party going on in there, and she's barred her guests from the kitchen. Somehow I doubt it. Though she has more of a spring in her step now.

I was in the living room yesterday, standing by the window, sipping a mug of tea, looking up the street. It was the very edge of dusk, the lights had just come on, the street, wet from the afternoon rain, glistening, and even here, in the heart of this grimy city, there was more than a hint of magic, when, looking down, I see her rounding the corner. And she didn't look quite so brown, somehow. In fact she was wearing a *black* leather jacket. Nothing particularly smart. Hardly Burberry. Probably picked up from the charity shop a couple of streets away. In fact, I remembered seeing one rather like it in the Cancer Care window last week. Had thought as I walked by: You'd better get your act together, fella. Or else, forget Hugo Boss, bye-bye John Smedley, Cancer Care is around the corner. You may have a book contract, but, these days, most book contracts aren't worth the paper they're written on. So don't go assuming you're the exception.

*

I know what they say about February, but, this winter, it hasn't got to me as it so often does; I can already smell spring in the air.

I went up to the park yesterday, as dusk was falling. The snowdrops are out, crocuses still pushing through. I've begun to make a habit of it: walking around the park. It lifts me. Two days ago I thought I saw him there – in the half-light, it was hard to tell. Anyway, he smiled as we passed each other, and I heard myself say, 'Good evening.' 'And what a lovely one it is.' I heard him reply as he strode on towards the gate.

He's not exceptionally handsome. Just nice-looking, in an honest, trustworthy sort of way. I'm glad about that. I know it makes no sense, but I am.

I haven't seen him quite so much this week. There's been more to do at the library. We've become the main *hub* for this area. They tell us this as if we should be grateful, as if it's a reward for services rendered, but really it just means we'll work a lot harder for the same money and, with a bit of luck, *won't* get sacked. Mustn't moan though. I need to keep this job for another decade or more, or else… Still, must *not* go there. Inch by inch, life's a synch. Yard by yard it's very hard. I have to chivvy myself along, remember to live in the moment. It helps. It's been my life's work: self-chivvying.

Lots of new things happening at The Hub – as we, jokingly, call our buzzing old workplace. We've a series of events coming up soon. I normally make a few preliminary phone calls, do some of the arranging, leave the usual time, and that's that. But last week, as I was distributing the new periodicals, Freda comes up to me and says, 'Megan! Fancy doing a bit of hospitality for one or two of these up-coming events? I know it's not your thing, but, who knows? You might enjoy it. And you get to hear the writers.' 'Why not?' I hear myself saying, 'Yes! OK.'

I thought, having agreed to it, I might find an excuse, might back out before time – as I did once before. But, so far, it hasn't happened.

*

As winter's turned to spring the Brown Woman's become less brown; I swear her hair has a glint of autumnal redness about it.

We passed in the street again last week – well, passed on opposite sides of the street. I waved, smiled silently. She did the same. She may've been coming back from the park. I was going up there, getting away from my desk, my computer. I've changed the setting for my emails: no more cheery little pings and red numbers flashing when Becky sends me another of her *I'm sorry* missives. I've got so I don't check my Inbox for days on end. It's quite liberating! Unfortunately Duncan doesn't give up. Just gets on the phone.

'Hey there, mate,' chirpily, at first, hoping the Mr Nice editor will get more out of me than Mr Nasty has to date, 'Gigi wants you to do a couple of gigs next month. Thinks that lovely profile of yours needs raising a bit. You up for it?'

The gap between books panning out to become what Duncan sees as a yawning void of three years, he's getting rather twitchy.

'Thought I was supposed to be keeping my nose *down*, Dunc, get the damn thing done.'

'Speaking of?' Duncan says, pretending he had no intention *of* 'speaking of', 'How is The Damn Thing?' adding dryly, 'Good macho title. Like that. So far, so good.'

'Oh,' I say, 'you know, not exactly flowing, but,' I lie, 'it's trickling along.'

'The Damn not *blocked* then?' he says, all chirpiness draining from his voice. 'Two or three chapters would be nice.'

'Do they have to be *nice* chapters?'

'Y'know, words, sentences, a few paragraphs on a few pages'll do fine. Electronic pages, you understand. Email me a doc asap. Thursday pm: i.e. before four. On second thoughts, make that three. I'm curling up by my Cheshire wood burner this weekend. Just me and my Kindle.'

Grant darling, Becky writes, *Can't we somehow work this thing out? I'm almost certain the baby's yours, not Harry's. Can't we just forget it ever happened? Because I almost have.*

Almost. Not once, but twice. *Almost.*

If you've managed to so completely fuck up your actions, Becky, *darling*, then do try not to fuck up your words too. *Almost* certain is *not* certain enough. Yet, I presume, you assume you have me over a barrel here; assume, if this baby's mine, I'll want it to have a good life, a family life. Even though you'd fucked that family up before it came into existence. You know something, Becks? I almost hate you.

*

My boy was born on May 10, 1974, I having been shipped away to a distant relative in time to save the family honour. Oh, the disgrace of it!

I don't suppose it was meant as cruelty. But neither was much kindness shown. Though my father, in those last few weeks before I was transported to Derbyshire – feeling branded, unclean – would, more frequently than usual, put his big, hard-skinned, workman's hand on my skinny shoulder and pat me gently as he passed by, saying nothing, my pale hand reaching up to lightly brush the tips of his blackened fingernails before he whisked them away.

'It's for the best,' all my mother could say, 'For the best.' If this is the best, I thought, whatever would the worst be like?

But, to my parents, the worst was *inconceivable*. And even if the shame of it could be tolerated, where was the money to come from for another child? I might have had a brother or sister of my own, had there been money for the luxury of children.

He was quite a long baby, his skin the colour of drilled soil that warm, waterless spring. His father's skin had been darker: humus rich, fertile, full of goodness – I thought. And maybe that was the case, since I have never been able to hate him. For what was there to hate? I suppose that had been part of the fascination, that difference: his drawling, relaxed voice, his coiled-sprung hair, the gleaming copper nut beauty of his skin. I had no fear then. I was bursting into life. Wanting, wanting, wanting.

'*Megan!*' my outraged mother cried, 'Whatever were you thinking of?'

I said nothing. Since she had never understood, never before enquired as to what I was thinking, why should she know now? Though if I had told her, I would have said: Mother, at the time, I was thinking of absolutely nothing. Was, for one brief, beautiful hour, one warm insect buzzing, bird-twittering, cricket-chirping September afternoon, so at one with nature, with my body and with his, that nothing else mattered. Nothing else at all.

I saw my baby for fifteen minutes. A kind nurse allowed me to hold him. 'Against the rules, really,' she said, laying the child in my child's arms. I was not supposed to 'bond' with him, you see, since this would make the situation more painful for me.

Until that moment, I was not aware anyone was much concerned with *my* pain. I kissed his damp forehead, whispered his name – the name I had given him – and cried.

Soon I was shipped back to a place that was now more alien to me than ever. Some cobbled together story was put about to cover my absence. Should anyone ask after my 'illness', I would nod and attempt a smile. Sometimes I would cry. This completing the picture of the vulnerable girl who had had a 'nervous breakdown'.

Returning to school seen by my mother as too big a reward for my sins, nothing was said on that score. I was given a job in the nearby canning factory, where I spent the next thirteen months shelling peas and washing carrots, until, finally, I left the place the fortunate fondly call home.

*

Duncan has gone apeshit. So apeshit he's forced to call me from his Cheshire wood-burnerside.

'Fireside, sounds so much cosier, don't you think, Dunc?' I say, warmly, before Duncan hits me with his fiery rage.

'Perhaps I should've dropped off the hard copy? Then you could've chucked it in there.'

'And I bloody would've,' Duncan growls. 'What the *hell* is this about? What's happened to the original synopsis? And, more importantly, where's our bloody hero? Does Darius Armstrong come into this strange story at *any* point?'

'What do you reckon?'

'Grant, you *cannot* do this. You're bloody *contracted!*'

'Sorry, Dunc. Killed Darius off. It was him or me. Happened off the page. Got no control over what happens off the page. Anyway, since *I* gave birth to him, don't I have the right to write him out of my life?'

'Are you sure,' Duncan says, 'going off piste like this is not more about your private life, about you and Becky, than any *real* desire to kill off D I Armstrong?'

'Certain, Duncan. Honest t'God. I'm feeling pretty sober about all that right now. I'm living like a monk, here in my little writing cell, and, y'know what? I am actually *enjoying* writing. Enjoying it more than I have in years. So, if you don't mind…?'

But Duncan's still grumbling on about me throwing the baby out with the bathwater. Speaking of which? If Becky finds out – and I wouldn't put it past Duncan to grass on me – *she'll* be on the phone soon, wanting to know where the money's coming from. Mortgage and rent for this place doable. But money for a baby? Then, come Monday afternoon, Gigi'll be breathing down my neck, pissed off with me for shuffling off the shelf she likes to keep me on.

'Come on now, Grant,' Duncan is saying, 'Just *one* more. Put this worthy stuff aside for a few months, kill Darius off in a big, block-busting final book, we bring out the boxed-set the following year, *then* you move on.'

'Sorry, Dunc. The man's dead. D-E-A-D, *dead*. He is an ex-protagonist. He is as stiff as your favourite Kindle. He will not rise up – whatever inducements you throw at me.'

Thing is, this… *little death* has got me out of the hole I've been in for years. For the first time in a long time I'm flying. Don't know what I'm doing, don't know where I'm going, don't need to – just yet. Just know I haven't written like this since way back. Know that, despite all the shit that's gone on in my life, I can still hack it – or rather, *not* hack it. I can sit in this room, looking out on those dreary grey walls, all those windows – most of them dark, most of the time, save for mine and the Brown Woman's – and *not* be in Grub Street, can transport myself to another world: a world where craft takes over from the market place – a place where I'm starting to feel quite at home.

'Inducements are thin on the ground right now, Grant,' Duncan informs me. 'As you well know. Literary fiction only *really* sells if you make the Man Booker, land yourself a big prize. Is that what your aiming at? Getting a gong before you hit forty?'

'Not aiming at anything, Dunc old mate. Just want to write well. Want to write a novel caring about every word that's in it.'

'Well, we're going have to re-negotiate your contract for that! Trust you're aware this'll change things, and not necessarily for the better.' A thoughtful pause follows, in which I am supposed to come to my senses. Then, 'How's Becky doing, by the way?'

I ignore this blatant attempt at emotional blackmail.

'Re-negotiate away, Duncan! Money's not everything, is it.'

'Isn't it?' Duncan says, hanging up.

It's been abnormally warm for early April. The other evening, my top sash pulled down, her casement opened wide, I hear cutlery clattering on the draining board up there, hear, post-clatter, her radio on: a concert on 3, the music wafting down. Schubert, I think. I flick on the radio I keep on my desk, but seldom listen to, stop working and just listen. I must've been blasting it pretty loud, too, because, when I look up, I see her looking down. I raise my hand in a thumbs-up gesture, and she gives me a double thumbs-up back. And I find myself feeling extraordinarily content. It was one of those sublime moments when the moment itself feels quite perfect. I completely forgot how shitty I'd felt after Becky's call. Why *should* I be at the birth? Does she think if she gets me there, whatever the outcome, she'll have me? Life's got to be more than duty, more than responsibility. Where's the passion in that? And perhaps, I've begun to think, it's got to be more than knowing. Or more than *thinking* you know. You see, I'm getting to like *not* knowing. Getting quite fond of this intuitive approach to my work – to life in general.

She's not been in quite so much over the past few weeks: the Brown Woman. I'm glad she's got more of a life for herself. Although I always like it, come the evening, when I look up and see a light go on up there, see her making tea, cooking, washing something in that sink. Funny that.

'Please, Grant. *Please* think it over,' Becky pleads.

'So,' I say, 'have you invited Harry along to this. . . big opening, too? Have you covered all the angles?'

'*Jesus, Grant!* I *told* you. Harry's out of the picture.'

'Completely out, or *almost* out?'

'You are so fucking. . .'

'Pedantic, I think you'll find the word is,' I say, and she hangs up.

Gigi felt the need to come round yesterday, brief me re my profile-raising gigs.

'Grant, whatever may or may not be going on in your head re Darius…'

'Never fear, Gigi,' I say, 'Nothing re Darius *is* going on in my head.'

'Whatever. Anyway… Just do this *one* incy-wincy thing for us, will you, Grant, sweetie? Just make like Darius has taken a holiday or something. Keep the punters interested. Right. Do *not* go saying you've killed him off. Not yet, Grant. OK. Budgets are friggin' tight, y'know. And *I* need my job, even if you don't need yours.'

I get the message and promise to be good.

*

There's quite a crowd at the library, quite a buzz. I start to get that tug-tugging feeling, that egoistic kick. See a few of my readers looking over to me, hear my name whispered behind one or two hands, and get quite a buzz myself.

I'm standing there, commanding my horned inner demons to back off, when this rather nice voice, soft but with a hint of huskiness, says, 'Would you care for a glass of wine?'

She's pretty slim beneath that earth-brown coat, that Cancer Care leather jacket, the Brown Woman. Close up, the face looking up at me looks a little younger than I'd thought. She's wearing a bit of makeup – all very subtle – a black top and a rather nice chunky necklace. And I don't know quite what to say to her, face to face, so I just nod, and she hands me a glass of red.

'I'm afraid I'm not a fan,' she says, 'I just work here.'

'Don't be afraid,' I say, 'Be proud. I'm sure you have much better taste.'

She doesn't assure me she has or has not, just says, 'I'm Megan, by the way.'

'Grant!' I say.

'I think I already know that, don't I?' she says, indicating the poster on the wall, 'Unless…? Is it a pseudonym?'

I shake my head.

After I've done my self-reverential spiel, signed a pile of books, sold a few, I notice she's still there, gathering up the glasses, collecting the bottles.

'Care for another?' holding up a half empty bottle of red.

'Any chance of a quick cup of tea?' I say, 'Throat's a bit dry after all that blah, blah-blahing.'

She tells me how good my blah-blah-blahing was, and I find myself telling her what I shouldn't tell her about the death of Darius Armstrong, and then, after standing there for half an hour or more, after topping up my tea, each of us, by now, perched on a table amongst the dishevelled chairs, the shelves of books, she says, 'I had a child once, you see. His father came from Louisiana. He was taken away… my baby. Well, I was only a child myself. It was just… you reminded me, you see… and I thought, I wondered… '

'When? When was this?'

'He would've been, will, I hope, be thirty-seven next month.'

'Me too!' I say. 'Except, for me, it's October.'

Her face flushing, she looks down. Then, looking up again, says, 'It wasn't that I thought you were… not that I even wanted him to be… it was… I don't know… '

'I know,' I say, 'I know.'

*

I know, he said, *I know,* his face looking down into mine with such kindness, such understanding.

A few days later, I'm turning my key in the front door, when I hear him, calling from across the street: 'Megan! I'm just off to the park. Fancy a walk?'

As we walk he tells me about his wife, about the baby due in two weeks time.

'And you know what?' he says, 'Right now, in spite of what I've said to her, in spite of the anger I've felt towards Becky for lying to me back then, for putting me in this position now, I find myself hoping this baby *isn't* mine. Find myself – even though Becky swears she and Harry are through – wanting it's skin to be as lily-white as Harry's. After all her lies, I actually want my wife to be lying to me now, because, deep down, whatever happens, I feel our marriage is over.'

I tell him he might feel differently when he sees the baby, might feel something for it – and for his wife again – whatever the child's colour? But he shakes his head and says, he's 'had enough of being a performing seal'. Then abruptly changing the subject, he says, 'Isn't Death and the Maiden sublime? Got myself a copy: Amadeus Quartet. *Beautiful!* Can't stop playing it,' shaking his head, smiling to himself, 'You know, if my mother was still around to hear me say that, she'd either be baffled or proud.'

'Maybe both?' I say.

We are approaching the café. He gestures over to the tables. I take a seat at one of them as he goes to get tea for us both. Then he comes back, sits down, and tells me the story of his life.

The Lesser God

Andrew Oldham

The pigs hawked and squealed as Thom smashed head first through the rotten wooden palings of their sty. The splaying mud scuttled the pigs. Thom pulled himself up onto his forearms; his head throbbed with a whining that he could feel through his hands as they sank deeper into the filth of the pen. The starlings lifted as the earth heaved up and down, the flock of black escaping the quarry blasting. There it was in his fingertips, the dull sound of the end for him and another part of the hill they lived on gave way to dust and shatter stone. He spat pig shit, one of his molars, grey, cracked and bloody lay in the dirt of the sty. Thom laughed at the stupid starlings and filthy pigs, at the shit and blasting; he could feel the stone ash on his tongue as he traced it along his gums to the empty spot towards the back of his mouth. The taste of copper, stone and pig. Thom rolled over, held out a hand to the man who took his tooth, Jakes.

Jakes stood fists bared, ready for Thom to get up. He was not stupid, Thom was a farmer and they always fought dirty against quarry men. Jakes kept a fist tight and relaxed the other to help Thom up.

Thom was up, face to face with Jakes, he was on his feet and he pulled back his fist. Then all went black, punctuated by the image of a crab apple tree, the fallen apples, the long grass and then mud folded around him once more, his tongue lolling back in his mouth flopping against the dead hole where his tooth was, his mouth, his skull pounding with the blood rising up to keep him weighed down.

Thom was all piss and blow.

One shilling. One shilling wasn't worth such a beating. Jakes looked down at Thom's body, his face swelling and the lump on his head where he'd demolished the pigpen was a livid colour, blackening before him. It wouldn't have been too bad if Thom had not shown up during Jakes dinner. It was brisket night, the one night of the week where he didn't have to eat pork. The one day when Fifika bartered for beef or fish, anything that didn't squeal and shit on him whilst he changed their bedding. Jakes would have wolfed down the brisket in his youth but now he was cracked, weathered and worn. The beef would be on the hotplate keeping warm and shrivelling to nothing.

Thirty years, and still they came to wrestle him, to try and best him, to figure out how a man in his fifties with a busted knee and bowed back from the tamping iron bested everyone. Jakes would think of himself as the tamping iron as he wrestled, slow and methodical he would work his way through a bout and strike only when he had to. There was nothing like the feel of the tamping iron slowing sinking into the stone. Twelve men in a row all with irons, working their way along a cliff edge, the breeze, the weather on their backs as they worked. And then the monkey men with their dynamite and wooden boxes, their fuses and timings, their maths and loud explosions that rang in their hands for weeks. Yet, before and after work, they would come to wrestle Jakes, many he had never seen before, many he knew and never saw again after he pinned them all and emptied their pockets. He was the wrestler, one shilling for a full wrestle, a penny for an arm wrestle. You put your money on the table and you took your chances. Jakes was known, heard of all over the hills, they'd come from Cheshire, Lancashire and Derbyshire to wrestle him, he'd even held a cockney and a Cornish man in a half nelson, and watched all of them limp off back to where they'd come from, penniless and broken. Jakes owned his own house, he was the only one in the hamlet to do so, he owned the meadow and the field that ran to the quarry. No one robbed him, no one crossed him and no one showed him lack of respect until Thom. There were other wrestlers who made their way in the world, but they charged pennies for half hearted fumbles in alleyways and pub yards. There was a woman in Slaithwaite by the name of Bess, she fought dirty by unbuttoning the top four buttons of her blouse. It was difficult to take down a woman like that without getting aroused. Jakes knew from his youth that even a few lasses gathered around to watch him wrestle would make him bend further, make him wait for the pin down as he fought off the girls around him. The one's who jeered, slapped his arse, felt his muscles, patted his chest and wanted more than one shilling's worth. Then there was Fifika. One day, twenty odd years ago, dark, small, quiet.

She did not jeer.

She did not slap him.

She did not show an interest in his muscles.

She married him.

A gypsy girl who came with the tinkers and never left.

Jakes tramped down the hill to the house where Fifika sat on a stool by an open window to the kitchen, her arms crossed, her lips turned down, a clay jar by her feet that he stooped to drop Thom's coins into. There were no words, she held out her hand to steady him as he climbed the stone lip of the window-sill and lowered his legs into the kitchen. He would have to fix the hole Thom has left in the pigpen after the beef.

The kitchen was steaming wet, the heat almost unbearable. Fifika followed him over the windowsill; he took her in his arms and lowered her to the flagstone floor. The briefest of touches from Fifika that he couldn't feel anymore. Then she was away into the gloom, a shadow against the roar of the range and the whistling of the kettle. The door to the front room was closed. He liked it that way. It kept out the worst of the intruders. Fifika emerged from the steam holding the remains of his brisket, a pale shadow of what it was, tough and leathery between his teeth, a piece of meat that squeaked on the plate as he sunk in his knife. He didn't have the heart to tell her that last week he'd lost all sense of taste. He tongue merely chafed his cheeks now.

Fifika looked up the garden as she retrieved the clay jar from the windowsill where she left it, that fool Thom was being picked up by two men, one on each side to steady the load. One was short, another farmer, she was in no doubt they were all short and black to the touch. They always brought the mud in with them and covered everything in her house. The second was tall and lithe, more willow than man, between them they struggled to pick up Thom. Fifika would have laughed but Jakes was tackling his steak like a man possessed and she was sorry that she could not cook. She was not her mother. Her mother who could cook from the hedgerows, pull plants from the ground, grow sweet and succulent things in the smallest of ways. Fifika was not that type of cook, it was brown or black, either way you ate it and got on with the day. She mustn't have been that bad, Jakes had never complained and neither had any of her children bar one. She watched the two men pull Thom between them and plough the ground with his trailing feet, one of them held up a hand, the short one.

'They're waving goodbye,' she said.

Jakes grunted, his mouth full.

'The short one waves.'

'John,' replied Jakes.

She laughed it was short and sharp it jangled the coins in the clay jar. It was obvious that the brothers didn't have the same father one was short, one was tall, one was balding and the other was just a fool. She wondered which one of the tinkers who passed this way had caught their mother.

'The pigs are loose,' she added at the end of the laugh. A full stop remark that Jakes nodded at 'Best fix it, can't have them out all night'.

Jakes looked up as Fifika moved towards the coalhole; even in the gloom he could see that she was wearing trousers under her skirt again. By the looks of it they were a pair of his old work pants. He didn't mind. Most men would have hit her, told her to be mindful of who she was and what she was. A gypsy. Jakes was not like most men, he looked down at his knife, at his hands and back at Fifika's swishing skirt and trousers as she pulled back a sack of coal, brushed back the coal dust and lifted a small sandstone flag. She pushed the jar into the hole beneath it and reversed the process, ending with the coal sack over the hiding place. She'd given him six children: two dead, three married, two with children of their own.

One shilling.

He sighed.

Jakes looked back at his hands and shook his head. Thom was a lousy bastard. He'd broken the rules and his pigpen. Jakes hadn't thrown the first punch. Jakes hadn't punched anyone since he was fifteen and that had been a horse. Wrestlers didn't punch it damaged the arms and weakened the shoulders. His father had told him that, drummed it into him as he taught him every move, every rule of the game. He'd draw chalk circles on the ground; show how points could be scored inside and outside the line. How some men used circles of grain, which was illegal and wasteful, grain shifted in the wind, grain cracked and rolled under foot. Grain could bring you down easily. Always wrestle inside the chalk lines, put your opponent outside them. The chalk line was your world. Rope was expensive but it gave and could be used with the right weight, the right slam but it was wasteful, it could catch you out, tie you in knots and rope around a group of losers is not good. Many a wrestler has been lynched because of rope rings. His father the wrestler, his grandfather a wrestler and so and so on and each had died wrestling, paupers dead in pub yards, beside canals, in factory loading docks, in ship holds. He watched Fifika as she pulled in the stool from outside.

'How much?'

'Just over now.'

Pence from arm wrestling, pounds from the rings, only chalk, never grain, never rope. Jakes nodded. He didn't know if that was enough or not. Fifika knew. She bought this house, the meadow and the field. Jakes wrestled. Fifika invested. Fifika would tell him when they had enough.

There it was from the other room.

Scraping along the foot of the door.

Fifika climbed out the window she didn't wait for Jakes to help her.

Jakes pulled out the key from his jacket pocket. The key was gnarled and rusting but it still did the job, it still turned the lock and slid back the bolts.

The room beyond was held in dusk, the roaring fireplace cast shadows that a child knew better than to dream of.

Two dead.

Three accounted for and married.

One left.

Never spoken about, no family, no friends uttered a single word about the one left.

Scarit.

The Lesser God.

Named itself.

Jakes looked down at it before scooping it up and placing it back in a chair by the fire.

Scarit.

From the start.

It had slid out of Fifika, stone cold, stone cawl, stone limbs and eyes.

One word.

Scarit.

They'd hidden him.

Scared of neighbours.

Scared of fire in the middle of the night.

She was gypsy. She was a witch. She'd never been trusted. Fifika.

'You win'.

It wasn't a question. Scarit knew he'd won. Scarit made him win. Scarit had suggested the one shilling a go. Eight years gone.

'Coal.'

This was the end of the conversation. Jakes grabbed the coalscuttle and left the room.

*

Jakes could see in the light from the bottom of the privy door. He was sweating as the cuts from the fight healed. Fissures in his skin sealed themselves over the stone beneath.

It was the deal taken eight years ago.

Jakes was more stone than man and it reminded him that he had an owner.

Jakes slammed a damp palm against the privy wall, left the print of his hand and pulled up his trousers, slapped the braces back onto his wet shoulders and kicked open the privy door. He needed to fix the pigpen, put back what Thom had broken. Jakes grabbed a hammer from the tool shed it was for show but everything in his life was. He wished he could feel the difference between the wood and the metal head of the hammer but there was nothing there, just the shape of a hammer with none of the memory of it.

Once he worked with twelve men on the cliff edge tamping iron into stone. He wrestled them all over the eight years.

He worked alone now.

The first dust motes of the evening where out as he tramped up to the pigsty. He flung the hammer down into the long grass it was there just in case a neighbour called around.

They never did.

Only those who wanted to wrestle came now.

In these moments he could let his strength have free rein;

let his hands do the work. He pulled a kinked nail from one of the wooden palings and rolled it between his palms. The metal started to glow and stretch as Jakes pushed out the creases. He spat in his hands, a great fat gob that sizzled as it hit the nail and cooled it enough to allow him to drive it on to the sty posts with the flat of his hand. Thom would never know how lucky he was.

*

Thom's jaw was swollen and the side of his head felt woolly. Thom sat amongst the laughter in the pub; all he had left was the dregs of a pint and the mockery of his so-called kith and kin.

'I told you,' said John.

'Well, you're too short to best him,' he replied, draining his glass and holding it up. The pub owner nodded, turned to an old timer at the bar whispered something in his ear. The old timer just turned, looked Thom up and down and shook his head. The pub owner joined in the head shaking as he pulled another pint of ale for Thom.

'I'd have lasted longer.'

His brother joined in the shaking of heads that echoed around the saloon, family, friends all turning their heads back and forth, back and forth. Thom couldn't stand it he pulled himself up and teetered, swaying in a sea of heads he pushed through them all, ignored the barking and swearing, the cat calls and horse kicks to his shins as he passed through. He ignored the pint on the bar with his name on it. He glared at the pub owner and the old timer and pushed open the door and staggered out into the night. The pint remained on the bar, a lace doillie placed beneath it.

Thom leant against the wall of the barn and looked over his fields. The cows were fat, his lips were fat, the cows shat and Thom looked away. A fag hung from the side of his mouth that wasn't swollen it fought for space against the blood blisters and spit. He couldn't see how an old man like Jakes could get the better of him. He was a farmer. He was a man of the land. He drove horses. Beat ploughs back to shape. Cut through the earth beneath his feet. Thom had bested the slut over at Slaithwaite. She'd unbuttoned her blouse but still went down like a turned sod. There were no hard feelings, she'd told him that later in bed but by the next morning she'd still gone off with Thom's wallet and trousers. He hadn't been angry at that. He'd won. He'd had his fun and he'd paid for everything he'd done that night. There was nothing in the wallet worth keeping and the lack of trousers hadn't raised an eyebrow back at the farm. There had been a few jeers but they had been more about being a lucky sod than a broken pony. Jakes worked the quarry, everyone knew quarry men ended up with bowed legs and broken backs. Thom should have beaten him with one hand tied between his arse cheeks.

When the wrestling began, Thom found out Jakes secret, the secret that those who fought Jakes in the past never told as no one would have believed them. It was the kind of secret sore losers spread. Jakes was heavy not fat. The kind of heavy that broke bones, that kept a man pinned to the mud with a simple push and roll. Thom shouldn't have punched him. He rubbed his jaw. Jakes had thrown a punch that would have buggered a beef cow. Thom had gotten a few blows in and now his wrists were running from sickly yellow bruises to deep purple black, his knuckles were bust open and gashes ran the length of his fingers. It was wrong. It was all wrong. Thom couldn't have won a straight wrestle with Jakes, the weight would have gotten him, no matter how much he twisted or tried to use Jakes' slowness to benefit him. It was the sheer weight.

*

John was found dead. The first leaves were falling and he had woken frightened and jabbering. He yelled about whispering, about stone. Then he'd walked out.

Hung himself.

Casting a length of rope down into the darkness of the old well.
His rough, small hands tying a knot to the winch.
Hoisting himself over, noose and all.
Falling like a sack, his neck cracking with the first jerk.
Thom's brother.
Bolshy bugger.
Cut off his own tongue.
Tore his ears off.
Clogged up his mouth and ears with cow shit.
Swung gently in the dark his feet inches above the water line.
The old timers came when he was dragged out. Flat capped and caned they wittered over walking sticks. His eyes bulged. His face was bloated, more bullfrog than man. Covered in snail tracks.

Now Thom was the man of the house, the last man of his family. He was solid when his Mother was told. Laid out the corpse on the kitchen table. Cleaned it up. Carried it in the coffin. Brought his sisters from Ashton. Took them back. Stood by the graveside. Never shed a tear. He strode around the hamlet, great steps that planted him firmly to the soil. He ploughed his fields with a new determination. Rebuilt dry stone walls that had lain fallow. Contained his grief. That is the story that the old timers spoke over pints of bitter.

But the night of whispers brought something different to Thom. Ploughing came easy. Dry stone walling wasn't a chore. He worked only with a hammer, no cloth to cover his hands. He worked and unlike before, he worked alone. His hammer discarded in the grass by the fallen stone.

*

Jakes' cough had gotten worse since the fight with Thom. Jakes had turned down a wrestle before breakfast citing rheumatism to a young man from Stalybridge. The man had left disappointed that the one man he wanted to wrestle wouldn't fight back. Fifika had caught the man as he left, asking if Jakes had offered an arm wrestle instead but the man had shrugged her off. He knew what she was.

Gypsy.

He spat in her wake.

Fifika caught Jakes coughing up blood in the privy, thick clots hung from his lips. He blamed it on the weather as he doubled over, letting out a spume that splattered the toilet bowl. He had tried to keep her out of the privy, hooking his great foot under the edge of the door barring her way but she was angry about the Stalybridge boy who had snubbed her.

Gypsy.

He had walked away ignoring her questions and she would be ignored by no man.

Fifika knew how to get into the privy one stamp on Jakes' foot and she was in. She knew he didn't feel it she knew his secret but she knew he still wanted to pretend. Fifika cradled him, her poor man, her poor husband she could feel the stone in his head. She held his cold hands and saw that his tongue, once pink, was now grey, now stone, grating against his warm bloody cheeks. He could not speak. He could not feel her. He missed her warmth. He missed her beside him in bed.

Thom's coming.

Scarit.

He tried to tell her but she would not let him go.

Thom.

Fight.

Money.

Reward.

Freedom.

Jakes pushed past her she could not hear the Lesser God she was free of his whispers. One more time and he would be free that was the promise. Scarit was giving him back his flesh. He left Fifika in the open privy doorway she watched him climb the hillside.

Fifika saw Thom climbing over the pigpen; saw how the planks gave under his weight. It echoed her husband. She wanted to call after him but neither man was now hers. She grabbed an empty potato sack from the store and climbed into the kitchen.

*

Thom stood in the mud of the pen, his weight sinking him down into the muck. The pigs were nowhere to be seen, the pen was empty. He slammed down his one shilling on the post, driving it down to the ground and embedding the coin in the wood.

'No refunds,' he spat at Jakes and launched into him, sending the old man sprawling.

*

Fifika unlocked the door to the parlour; she had stolen the key as she cradled Jakes. The Lesser God was there, whispering in his chair.

*

Jakes lay in the long grass as Thom stepped over him. Jakes' eyes were swollen, his jaw full of blood he sunk back into the grass leaving hardly an impression.

*

Fifika made her way up the hillside, the potato sack dragging by her side. It flattened the grass as she pulled it up the hill. Fifika knew a liar. Fifika always knew the Lesser God was one.

'It lies,' she had told Jakes.

He would not listen.

Eight years she had been silent, more statue than woman. Silence afforded her time to make plans and this had always been the last plan. The Lesser God didn't matter it could take its money she had not forgotten the clay jar it was there in the dark sack beside it. He would not be cheated this way.

The signs were new they had been placed closer to the house than last time. The quarry edge was close. There was no sound of hammers or of the tamping irons breakfast was long gone and she knew the routine of the quarry. Thom would come she didn't need to listen to the incessant chattering from the sack.

'Scarit. Dead. Dead as you will be. Scarit.'

It wasn't a name. It was the sound it made as it gulped, as it drew breath into its body, over dry lips that clicked and ground together each time it spoke.

'Scarit. Gone. Dead. Dead in the grass.'

*

Thom made his way up the ravine; the bottom of it was covered with slurry from the quarry, a thin brown drool of a stream that splashed as he strode through. Fifika was on the hill beside the quarry, she was cornered, she was on the edge, she would fall and it would be a dreadful thing. Fifika the woman who killed her husband then killed herself. Thom would be the one to find Jakes. Someone else could find the broken body of the woman. She had touched Scarit; she had taken what was his.

Scarit would leave with Thom.

It was all promised to him.

Scarit.

*

Fifika stood a few feet from the edge of the quarry she could see the fresh holes in the hillside, the snaking wires amongst the long grass. The monkey men had been. Below she could see them scurrying, the men who ate the hillsides, made warning signs. Given time they would eat the whole hillside, the valley below and the house were they had lived. Nothing would be left. It would all be eaten away by the dynamite and men with hands coarse as the stone they pulled from the earth. Fifika placed the sack by one of the dynamite holes.

Thom was coming.
The Lesser God was quiet.
Thom was here. The blasting siren was whining.

The Coroner's Report

Victoria Heath

Across the lawn, an elm tree's shadows took the shape of a man reaching out to strangle a woman. It was getting dark and the Coroner should have drawn the curtains, but the figures shook in the wind and caught his attention. He leant his weight onto the edge of the cold steel sink and watched the man thrusting his spiky hands towards her elongated neck.

'Could you close the curtains, please?' Emily sounded tense.

The Coroner pulled them to and turned to see his wife laying stems of winter honeysuckle across the kitchen table. 'Are they from the garden?'

'Yes. Beautiful, aren't they? It's starting to blow out there. Really chilly.'

He walked over to her side and stroked her upper back. He wanted to embrace her cold body and warm it with his, but she moved away, around the table to the cutlery drawer where she took out a pair of pink-handled secateurs.

'I've got so much to do,' she said and smiled fleetingly as she started to chop at short sprigs of the flowers. 'Could you light the fire in the lounge, please?'

The Coroner walked slowly to the drawing room and leant against the doorframe. He needed to use the bathroom before he set to work. Climbing the stairs he wondered what he would discuss over dinner. Perhaps the sudden heart attack of the local butcher that was causing him difficulties in his report; his guests could shed some light on the impenetrable matter, perhaps, perhaps. He shook his head, smiled and flicked on the bathroom light. In the brightness of the mirror his dark hair and pale complexion looked deathly. It surprised him, as it did from time to time, how like a coroner he appeared: tall and serious.

'Undetermined death,' he said into the mirror and watched his mouth dryly form each syllable. 'Heart attack aggravated by an abrupt change in temperature. Perhaps.'

When it came to the court hearing, there could be no ambiguous turn of phrase at the end of his statement. People expected a resolved judgement from his lips and he despised offering undetermined cause as a resolution. He turned and walked out of the bathroom and down the stairs.

Emily had been correct in thinking the drawing room needed heat. The Coroner quickly drew the curtains across the tall Georgian windows and crouched down in front of the hearth. The brass handle of the small hearth brush chilled his palm as he swept the cold ashes across the marble into a neat pile. He stood up and walked around his high-backed Chesterfield to pick up the log basket. It had not felt this heavy when they had first moved to this house and started using the fire. How many years ago was that? Fifteen? No, three years before Abbie's birth, so eighteen years. He was stronger then. A mere doctor at Hayfield Hospital, but a man without the stresses and tiredness of the position of a full-time Coroner. He set the basket on the sheepskin rug in front of the fire, pulled out a folded newspaper and rolled a long sausage shape with each sheet, in the way his father had taught him. He twisted each one into a knot, before laying it in the grate. Some kindling and two dry logs made for a strong fire. Placing the basket back in its position, he reached for the box of matches stashed behind the Cherry Boy statue on the mantelpiece, then struck a match and held the flame close to a paper end in the grate. The paper quickly disintegrated in the flames, which rose up and licked against the edges of the kindling, charring the sticks and eating into the wood grain. On Monday he had smelt this same charred stench on the Pathologist's table. The Coroner had not been able to visit the place of death; it was unstable according to the Chief Fire Officer. As an alternative, he had met with the Pathologist for an examination of the deceased. Inhalation of smoke and carbon monoxide. Global charring. Extensive thermal burns. Crush injury, left chest. Origin of fire yet to be determined. So many of the bodies he had presided over displayed similar causes of death.

'That's a strong fire,' Emily said.

The Coroner had not heard her come in. She carried four upturned sherry glasses, which they only used with company. Both he and Emily preferred gin.

'Come sit for a minute,' he said.

Emily smiled and placed the glasses on the coffee table. She stepped towards him, but a faint noise beeped through the wall.

'The potatoes!' She darted over to the door. 'Darling, could you set the table please?'

The Coroner smiled, but she left too quickly to see. He heard her footsteps click hurriedly across the black and white hallway tiles. The beeping stopped. He stood up and walked into the hallway. It felt cool in comparison to the heat that had risen through the drawing room and he tucked his hands under his armpits. The dining room felt equally cold and he checked the radiator to see if the warmth from the Rayburn had reached it, then edged up the temperature dial.

The room was too dark to set the table; he moved over to the doorway and flicked on the light switch. A second passed before the electricity met with the bulb. It was an incredible invention, electricity. Though his case on Tuesday may not have agreed. That benevolent young girl, who had stopped to help a distressed old woman, would never have had the chance to consider the fantastic power of electricity – as it pulsed through the fallen cable that blew into her left arm, causing fatal injuries throughout her body.

'Have you set the table yet?' Emily called out.

'In the process.'

The Coroner let his hand drop from the light switch. He turned and looked across the room at the bare tabletop. It called out for a body. To position an extinguished life on that sleek mahogany would have been appalling. Though the thought of Harriet Marsden's response as she walked through the dining room doors later in the evening – now that could be a compelling argument for such psychosis. On Tuesday evening the Coroner had stood over the stainless steel table as the Pathologist inspected the body of that electrocuted girl. Her engagement ring had melted into her hand and her eyes had been unrecognisable; the iris and pupils clouded into the sclerae. The current had puckered deep lines into her flesh, and had penetrated the majority of her organs. She did not represent an ideal image of peace in death. Harriet's continually jovial mouth would certainly droop at the sight of the crystal chandelier illuminating that acutely burnt corpse.

The Coroner ran his fingertips over the Edwardian dining table, given to them by Emily's mother the day after their honeymoon, twenty-nine years and eight days before.

'You haven't got the cutlery,' Emily said, walking into the room. She closed her eyes and shook her head. Her small black curls swung beautifully from side to side. She put an armful of silver cutlery wrapped in a tea towel gently onto the table, then stepped closer and put her arms around his waist.

'It's okay. I'll help. The lamb's in the oven with the roasties, the veg is prepped. There's not a lot else for me to do until they get here.'

They set the large table in silence. Each fork, knife and dessertspoon gleamed after she'd polished it delicately with a tea towel. She was so meticulous with every placing; each piece of cutlery pushed with the tip of her thumb to an inch from the table edge, and the four plates he put down she neatly edged into line too. In college she'd been the most orderly and well-presented student. As a housewife and occasional physiotherapist, she hadn't let this talent slip. Perhaps, looking through their house, another would consider the piles of books in the guest room ungainly, but they were merely pausing on their journey to the un-constructed bookshelves in the upstairs hallway – and she had carefully ordered each pile by genre and title. Every ounce of her behaviour was organised and balanced.

'I forgot the flowers,' she said.

'I can get them for you. Are they still in the kitchen?'

'Thank you. Yes, on the table.'

The Coroner entered the warm kitchen and thought of his wife in the dining room, intricately folding serviettes. Separation from her made his chest ache and he rubbed at it with his wrist. The honeysuckle stems were neatly arranged in the centre of the table, erect in three blue jam jars with tiny wire handles. He bent close and inhaled the scent. It was not as he had expected, more overpowering than the aroma of honey. It reminded him of something. What? He drew in the smell a second time and remained close, bowed over the table. *What?* A warm night. That was it: the new Detective Constable – with a tight brown perm and sharp features – who had greeted him at the gate of 54 New Dorset Street on Monday. Police cars congested the driveway, so he had parked on the kerb. As he stepped out of the car the woman had shaken his hand firmly. Her perfume, mixed with the heat of the evening, had irritated his nasal passages. This was the smell. As she led him through the bungalow, he could see three more police officers leaning against kitchen cabinets at the end of the hallway. He'd recognised two of them; time as a Coroner brought about many acquaintances who worked in the force. The Constable stepped aside to allow him passage and there he saw the trainers of a fifteen-year-old boy. He had fallen under the table and lay prostrate on the blue Formica tiles. The Coroner had known immediately from the pool of blood that a Laryngotracheal injury was clearly the cause of death. The boy's upturned face was still warm; he felt almost alive, dead just two hours.

'Darling,' Emily called from the other side of the house. 'Have you found the flowers?'

The Coroner straightened his aching spine and put his fingers through the wire handles of the jam jars.

'On my way!'

Emily was seated in the carver chair at the head of the table closest to the door. She watched him place the jars carefully in the centre.

'You've arranged them beautifully,' the Coroner said.

'I saw the idea in Ideal Homes magazine. Do you remember, I showed you on Monday?'

'No, I don't seem to recall that.'

She looked at him intently, then turned her head towards the open dining room doors. As she turned back she shivered and rubbed her arms briskly. 'The house is freezing tonight.'

'Yes, there is a bit more of a draught than usual.'

'I must have left a window open.' She started to stand, but the Coroner touched her shoulder lightly.

'You've worked tremendously hard on the meal,' he said, 'why don't you relax for a few minutes? I can see to it.'

She was so incredibly beautiful, but she looked tired. It was such a long while since they had entertained, and this first visit from the Marsdens would be sure to cause a stir – the couple were certain to report back to the rest of their friends on the evening's events. Everything had to be seamless.

'Where's Abbie?' he said, suddenly realising he hadn't seen his daughter all evening.

'She's gone to Tilly Green's house, with Isabella. They're having a sleepover.'

'Didn't they want to eat with us?'

'The Greens?'

'Abbie and Isabella.'

'They're fifteen darling. They want to *chill* in Tilly's boat house and talk about boys.' Her cheeks rounded as she smiled and rolled her eyes.

'But shouldn't she be here?'

'You know what she's like at the moment. She just needs a bit of time to herself.'

The Coroner glanced at the four table settings and stood up. As he walked upstairs, he wondered when he had last set a place for his daughter at the dinner table. He paused on the landing and looked out of the vast window, trying to see the tree where Abbie's swing had hung when she was younger. Only his reflection stared back, hovering in front of the rocking chair and grandfather clock. He shook his head and continued along the landing into their bedroom. The moonlight shone in through the open window and lit up the room with a white glow. The Coroner sat on the bed in the semi-darkness and unlaced his shoes, then stood, turned on the bedside light and opened his wardrobe. Smart jeans and a green pullover would be acceptable, with the shirt and tie he already wore. He unzipped his suit trousers and slipped his feet from them, sat on the bed again and started to pull on the navy jeans. But something on the carpet caught his eye. He leaned over for a closer look and rubbed his finger across a brown blotch in the fibres. *Never buy a cream carpet* were his mother's words when she had first visited their marital home. She had been correct in her thinking. Cream carpets always found themselves drawn to bright substances: Play-Doh, felt-tip pen, carrot soup, red wine, vomit, blood. In all the homes he had visited, the families would never entirely eliminate those constant reminders from the spot where the victims' bodies had rested. Whether it followed a natural death or something more sinister. The aftermath of that large cocktail of benzodiazepines and tricyclic antidepressants that had, so it appeared from the contusions on either side of the young girl's jaw line, been administered unwillingly. She was just two years older than Abbie, and had a similar sense of fashion. He felt a chill around his knees, lifted himself from the bed and buttoned his jeans. Before closing the door, he looked back at the bed and longed to retire, with his wife nestled beside him. But instead an evening of joviality was due to commence, full of the Marsdens' comments on the beautiful flowers in the garden and the delightful meal Emily had prepared – devastatingly simple courteous exchanges.

Each step of the stairs cracked with his weight as he headed down to Emily. At the bottom he listened carefully for her movements, yet heard none. He entered the sitting room, but the fire burned alone. He listened again then walked to the kitchen expecting her to be preparing the meal. But the lights were out and the room smelt of roasted meat rather than her perfume.

'Emily?' the Coroner called out, as he rubbed his chest quickly with his wrist.

'I'm in the dining room!'

She was seated in the carver chair at the head of the table closest to the door. 'You've changed your clothes again,' she said. He could see uncertainty in her dark eyes, but she smiled. 'Well, only three quarters of an hour till they arrive.'

'Emily, I'm so sorry,' the Coroner said, twisting his wedding ring round his finger as he spoke.

'What's wrong?' She shifted in her seat.

'Nothing's wrong. Don't worry.'

'What is it then, darling?'

The Coroner sat down in the chair to her left. 'The office called while I was upstairs.'

'I didn't hear the phone ring.'

'They said that I have to go in again. A body has been found on Montpellier Terrace. Quite possibly the result of a mugging.'

Emily reached her hand across the table and stroked his arm.

'How awful,' she said. He felt her fingers tighten.

'I should think Matthew and I will be able to form our conclusions fairly rapidly though, so I may be home in time for dessert.'

She blinked several times, as basal tears clouded her eyes. He smiled at the intricate workings of her most striking features, but didn't say any more. The curtains were moving weakly in the draught from the old windows.

'I love you so much.'

He looked from the curtains to Emily's hand on his arm. 'I love you, too.'

Emily stroked her fingers across his cheek.

'I must get my bag,' he said and stood.

He felt her follow him out of the room, and as he walked steadily up the stairs he could feel her watching. At the landing he stopped and turned to look at her, but she had gone from view. The clicking of telephone buttons sounded from the breakfast room, and after a moment he heard her speaking softly.

'Harriet? Hello, it's Emily. I am so sorry for the late notice, but I don't think Anthony is up to the dinner this evening... No, I think it's maybe still too soon. I am so sorry to do this again...'

The Coroner looked down at his hands as he listened. A small yellowish bruise had appeared on his wrist and he ran his fingers across it. Contusions around both wrists, right forearm and right upper forehead. He continued along the landing to the bedroom. Through the window, he could see the almost full moon hovering in the darkness. He sat on the edge of the bed. Multiple heavy contusions (and minor abrasions) across thorax, costal margin and upper abdomen. Pulmonary embolism due to multiple blunt force injuries.

Emily appeared in the doorway and flicked on the light. She looked startling in her black dress and matching heels, and he watched her glide towards the bed. As she turned and sat beside him, a brown stain on the floor caught his eye. He leant forward and scratched at the mark on the carpet.

Kowalski

Garrie Fletcher

Clearing a route to the window he shuffled over and sucked in the sweet scent of summer, or was it the black bin bags? Down on the street, kids kicked a ball against a neighbour's car. There was a time when he knew everyone in the street. He'd known their names, their jobs, their hopes, but they'd all gone. Moved on, just like her. He turned from the window as shouts erupted below, threats of repair bills and worse. He stared at the picture, the one that kept guard above the fireplace. A second of captured light, the white borders beginning to yellow. *'Katarzyna?'* She'd become a question that could never be answered. *'Pure, pure Katarzyna.'*

He slumped into the bags. Bin liners fat with newspapers, three deep and three high at the back with bags either side for an arm rests. He picked up the carburettor from the floor, held it close, and finding the fuel valve, inhaled deeply.

Katarzyna had laughed at his tinkering, saying he spent more time with his hands on engines than on her. She'd called him a fool when he said they reminded him of her, but it was true. Their first embrace was in the burnt out shell of a T-34. It was still warm. They'd clung to each other in desperation, two kids terrified of dying, horrified at living. As they clawed at each other the pungent aroma of fuel and sodden earth overpowered him. They made their way across a battered Europe, picked their way through the rubble of liberated nations until they came to Dover, Great Britain.

'Great Briton,' he said, then erupted into a choking laugh as he shuffled through the boxes and bags to the bathroom. The blind in the window cut strips of sunlight across the room, dust danced between the boundaries, swirling from light to dark and back again. He stared in the mirror as the water ran. An old man stared back at him.

*

'Mr Kowalski!' A fist hammered on the front door. 'Mr Kowalski!'

'OK, I come.' He climbed down the stairs, one hand clamped to the handrail whilst his feet searched for gaps in the bags. He pulled the front door open, squeezing more bags behind it.

'Bloody 'ell, Mr K, when are you going to clear some of this crap out?'

'When she comes. And is not crap, is my life.'

'Hell of a life.'

'Yes?'

'A letter for you.' He handed him a slim brown envelope with a bright recorded delivery sticker on it.

'And for this you break my door? What is wrong with letter box?'

'You have to sign for this, Mr K. Look, just here on this screen.'

Kowalski pushed the device back towards the postman, 'No, is not signature, is box with light.'

'This is how we do it these days Mr K, all high-tech.'

'I don't care how high, is not signature, goodbye.' He went to close the door.

'Wait, it could be important, it looks important, it's from the council.'

'Ha! Council,' he spat, then slammed the door.

Yesterday's coffee was flicked out of a cup and rinsed under the tap. He put the kettle on the gas ring, dried the cup on his shirt, then took a filter paper off the washing line hanging from the ceiling and fitted it into the cup.' Ha! Council,' he laughed as he loaded the paper with coffee grounds.

Kowalski sat on the back step, his feet on the cobbled alleyway, coffee cooling in his hand. The bags smelt stronger out here. Some had holes bitten in them, their contents scattered along the narrow gaps between. Down the alleyway, a group of kids on pushbikes wobbled towards him. They looked about ten or eleven and had a smaller kid running along behind them trying to keep up. They were all boys, brown skin, black hair, perfect smiles, hungry eyes. They started to giggle as they got closer, their legs working frantically on the pedals, building up speed, wired tight.

'Hurry up, Kassim, he'll get you,' the lead boy shouted.

'Slow down, you're too fast,' said Kassim, flushed with exertion, a sheen of sweat on him. The bikes flashed past Kowalski.

'Polski, polski, shit shop!'

'Go back to Poland and take your crap with you!'

'Polish go home!'

Kowalski leapt, grabbed the straggler by the arm and shouted, 'Why you abuse me? Why your friends tell me to go home?'

'Let me go!' shouted Kassim. Kowalski's grip held.

'No. You answer me. What have I done to you? Eh?'

Kassim's pupils grew bigger. Kowalski had seen eyes like that before. He loosened his grip.

'Tell me. What have I done to you?' Kowalski continued.

'They don't like you.'

'Why?'

'Because you're not from here, because you're foreign.'

'Pah. I built this city before your parents were babies, I'm as British as any of you.' He let Kassim go. The boy stood there, shaking. 'You like cricket, yes?' said Kowalski. Kassim nodded at him, his feet slowly moving backwards. 'When England and

Pakistan play who do you support?'

'Pakistan, of course.'

'Pah, and you're more British than me?'

'Well, who do you support?'

'I don't like cricket. Is girls' game.'

Kassim stepped backwards.

'Is OK. I won't hurt you. Tell your friends to leave me alone. I'm fed up of their insults.'

The small boy turned and ran as fast as he could up the alley to where his friends were waiting and shouted over his shoulder, 'Cricket's not a girls' game!'

Kowalski lifted his coffee up to his lips. 'Pah, cold.'

*

Kalisz was a beautiful city, one of the oldest in Poland. They'd ran raw through the markets, seeking excitement and adventure down the alleys and riverbanks, laughing at anything, with nothing but the weather to stop them. Then before they knew it, soldiers came to Nowa Street and they were stopped from playing there. On the one occasion they dared to sneak back they found that their friends were no longer there.

*

The back yard was filling up. Black bags were stacked three deep in some places along with bits of abandoned machinery. A rusted mangle poked through a tower of cardboard boxes, an old television, smashed, valves exposed, a couple of car wheels and in the corner near the outside toilet, a bike. Kowalski wrestled it free from the debris.

'Ah, there you go.' He held it up to the light and squinted at it as he talked to himself, 'Hmm, rust, bad spokes, nothing serious.' He carried it inside the house and slammed the door behind him.

*

Days crawled on. Heat, trapped by a blanket of cloud, opened all the windows along the street. Leaves began to burn at the edges and the grass that grew between the cracks in the pavement, turned transparent and died. The children ran less now, unless an ice-cream van caught them in its wake. They flopped in the shade, bike wheels spinning as they dreamt of the sea.

He went to the park. The stench in the house had become too much for him. The shallow, concrete pond splashed with children. A black dog chased its tail while most people clung to the dusty shade beneath bleached trees. Kowalski sat on a bench in direct sunlight. A dark shadow, from the brim of his hat, fell over his face. He wished he hadn't worn his jacket, yet it didn't seem right coming to the park without it. What would Katarzyna have thought?

The bike gang flew past, a jet stream of abuse. He looked, and sure enough Kassim was running after them. Kowalski squinted. 'Why you follow them, boy?'

'They're my friends.'

'Hmm, you can't get better friends these days?'

'What do you mean?'

'They never wait, or give lift?'

Kassim stared. Kowalski may as well have been speaking Polish.

'Come, see me tomorrow. I have something for you.'

'I'm not supposed to talk to strangers.'

'Are we strangers? You know where I live, you know my name.'

'I don't know your name.'

'Of course you do.'

'No I don't.'

'Polski Shit Shop, yes?'

'I can't.'

'Look. Just knock door and stand in street. I bring it out to you. Ok?'

'Spose.'

'Good.'

Kassim shuffled off after the disappearing bikes.

'Boy.'

He half turned, ready to sprint.

'My name is Kowalski.'

*

That night he was woken by the memory of rain and faint squeaking. It sounded like a dog playing with a toy but he knew better than that. *'Hmm, where is cat? Is cat's job.'* But the cat was long gone.

He waded towards the window trying not to notice the dark fluff that scuttled near the skirting. The city radiated an orange heat; streetlights bruised the sky, a hint of cloud. The overpass hummed in the distance, an ominous rumble, the echo of tanks. The war had come as storm clouds on the horizon, bursting closer and closer. Katarzyna dragged him into the field, her hair unfurled, his hand tight in hers. They heard soldiers and hid in the burnt-out tank, fear stretched tight across their throats. The night passed and in the morning, when they were sure they were alone, they carefully unbuttoned their clothes, hung them as neatly as they could and watched. Watched as every breath and beat brought them closer together, surrendered as they lost themselves in each other, every kiss and caress a cry for help, a cry for life.

Picking their way through the mud and bodies, the shattered trees, the exploded earth they made plans to leave Kalisz.

*

Kowalski stood in the yard. The bike looked good. He'd cleaned the rust off easily with some old wire wool and a half tin of Brasso, the brakes now firm and the chain well oiled. *'Hmm, is good bike,'* he thought to himself. The bike sat in the hall, propped against some boxes, for over a week.

*

'Morning Akram. How much is milk today?'

'Same as yesterday.' The shopkeeper looked into his newspaper for help.

'Pah, you bleed me dry, every day, bleed me dry.' Kowalski smiled.

'And you want everything for nothing.'

'Have not seen bike kids. You see them?'

'Kids? There's kids all over the place, with their thieving hands, bastard parents never beat them. They rob me blind!'

'Oh yes, beating, beating always works.'

Akram eyed him from over the top of his newspaper.

'Yes, beatings work wonders that's why we have no more fighting now, yes?'

'Piss off old man before your milk curdles.'

'Ah, you kind man Akram.'

He left the heady smell of cardamom, gram masala and spilt fizzy pop behind him, walked down the street, hugging the shade.

*

Sky torn apart. White blasts of cloud. Heavens on fire, blast after blast, drums pounding in the guts of the earth. Wave after wave from the sky, the very firmament against them, God's wrath in all its terror and glory, tearing the world asunder. And then, a slight lull until in the distance they scutter, insect chatter, as tracks roll on cobbled roads, down alleyways and streets heralding the screaming, the shelling, the dying…

He fell out of bed shouting, his fall broken by a large collection of *People's Friend* magazines and free newspapers. The window frame rattled from a blast as he picked his way across the room. Electric sky stabbed white; a deep boom rocked the house. He pulled open the sash window. 'Rain, rain!' Kowalski shouted at the storm, his fear fading. He skipped down the stairs nearly tripped then rushed out into the street, arms held aloft, letting the rain run over him, soaking his vest and shorts. His fine hair matted flat upon his skull; vest tight against bony frame, shorts in danger of becoming obscene. He started to laugh and dance, laugh and dance like he used to with Katarzyna, like he used to when she was alive.

*

The storm had washed away the dust. He bagged up more parts of his life and stacked them in the yard. The heat returned.

Kowalski sat out on his front wall. Flies hovered over him, sharing the shade from the large oak. The storm a dream now, the tree roots knuckling up at the memory of it. He pulled the peak of his Trilby down, felt decadent wearing just a vest with trousers, but the heat was intolerable and Katarzyna was not here to complain. He heard the bikes before he saw them, the frantic whirr of cog and chain, playing cards fixed into spokes, flapping, flicking as the wheels span round.

'Kassim, Kassim, Kassim,' they chanted as they shot down the street and sure enough, he came stumbling along.

'Polski, Polski, shit shop!' they shouted. Kassim stopped in front of Kowalski, his breathing ragged.

'Ah, your friends, still with the funny jokes and you still with no bike.' He stared at him. 'Wait there, big man, I get you a glass of water.' Kassim sat on the wall, legs dangling. 'Here you go.' Kowalski walked out with a glass of water in one hand and a child's bike in the other.

'What's that?' asked Kassim.

'Is glass of water, you not see before?'

'No, not that. That?' Kassim pointed at the bike.

'Oh, is bike. I'm throwing it out, is too small for me. Here.' Kassim gulped the water as he focused on the bike. 'You try?' The boy dropped off of the wall and stepped back. 'Is Ok, bike won't bite. What you afraid of, is only bike?' Kassim looked up and down the street, then put his hand on the handle bar. 'Go easy on front brake, is a little sharp, I need to adjust.'

At first he wobbled, fighting gravity, each push on the pedal swinging him from one side to the next and then, he was off.

Down the street, across to Akram's, then back, his whole body panting with pleasure.

'You ride well for cricket lover. You keep.' Kassim leapt away from the bike. 'What is wrong? You have bike, is too small for me.'

'I can't.'

'Why?'

'I can't take things from a stranger.'

'Well don't take then, just borrow.' Kowalski turned and walked back into his house. When he looked out at the street both Kassim and the bike were gone.

*

Boom, boom, boom. Metal on wood, metal against metal, and then nothing.

*

Kowalski woke late the next day. He looked at the gunk in the sink and made a mental note to get washing up liquid as well as something to eat. Down the hall, a halo of light burnt behind the stained glass at the top of the doorframe. Katarzyna had loved that glass. It was the first thing she noticed about the house, the first thing that made her fall in love with it. He pulled back the door and stepped out. Stepped out onto the mangled frame of a bike.

'I don't understand, Akram. I give boy bike and next day bike is fucked against my door, what is wrong with the world? What is wrong with the world that a kid would do that, that a kid would do such a thing?'

Akram busied himself behind the counter of the shop. He moved packets, that didn't need moving, stacked newspapers, that didn't need stacking and checked his mobile phone that was neither ringing, nor vibrating. 'I don't think the kid did it,' he said at last.

'What?'

'I don't think the kid did it?'

'How you know.'

'Just leave it. Maybe you should go away for a few days?'

'Why? So you can rob my house?'

'Yeah, and steal all your jewels.' Akram shifted the newspapers again. 'Seriously, go away for a few days.'

'I don't want to go away, why would I go away? I like it here, here is where I live.'

'Is that it?' Akram looked at Kowalski's shopping.

'What happened? What happened for you to say such a thing?'

'The boy's brother was in here.' Akram avoided eye contact as he stabbed at the till, 'he was in here asking after you.'

'I don't live here?'

'He was asking about you, what you were like, where you live.'

'And?'

'You don't argue with Mohammed.'

'Everyone called Mohammed. What is it with you people?'

'I'm serious. You should go away.'

Kowalski walked home.

He stood outside the house. The house they settled in, the house that she loved. The house she said they would never leave. He looked up and down the street. Despite the heat he felt a chill, something he hadn't felt since Europe. The Yale key clicked in the lock. He pushed hard on the door whilst speaking to himself, deep, measured, 'No more running, no more. Home Katarzyna, home.' In the kitchen he put his shopping away and lit the kettle.

Clarrie and You

Elizabeth Baines

Often when you think of Clarrie, you see her in her bright-green swimsuit, fifteen years old, an Amazon mermaid picking her way across the rocks towards the sea, hands flapping like flippers already, the sea and sky behind her a freshly-painted backdrop. She would get to the place where the rocks fell away in a cliff-face just beneath the water, a place where you, the smaller younger sister, would never dare go because you couldn't swim, and she dived. Then there she was, way out, her white cap bobbing, as if she'd forgotten the world on the shore.

You were jealous, of course.

Or you think of her earlier, leaping the glassy puddles in the lane to your gran's where you'd often be sent for the day. She seemed to fly; she'd take off on her muscular legs – sure-footed, never landing in cowpats – then run, leaving you to pick your way around the pools, afraid of the ghost dog someone had seen by the stile and desperately hoping she'd stop to watch a bird. She knew the names of all the birds, Clarrie, the little dull ones that most people don't even know are different from each other. She knew all the flowers; she could identify every variety of tree.

Not that many people would know: in school she never opened her mouth. She was big and she was strong, but she was cripplingly shy. In company she'd hang back, saying nothing. People thought she was stupid, when really she just wasn't very worldly-wise.

'Look after Clarrie,' your mother would tell you quietly before the two of you went out together – you on your spindly legs and not even coming up to Clarrie's shoulder, and Clarrie most likely to shoot off without you the moment you were out of sight.

There are things you don't want to remember, because doing so makes you guilty, after all these years and at your time of life, of ridiculous sibling rivalry. The way that sometimes, when Clarrie's friend Minnie went with you to Granny's and however hard you begged they wouldn't let you play, Granny would take Clarrie's side.

You'd dance around her pleading: 'Please, Clarrie, *please!*' but she wouldn't answer, she turned away, her shoulders set, stubborn and resentful, and in the end Granny would tell you off: 'Leave Clarrie alone.'

Clarrie was Granny's favourite. 'She's one of us,' Granny would say, by which she meant big like Granny herself and everyone else on your father's side. And of course, at ten years old, you were jealous of *that*.

You'd insist, full of injustice and a sense of exile: 'But I want to play!'

'It's not always what *you* want,' Granny would tell you. 'Don't be so selfish.'

And Clarrie would sit silent, and Minnie, censorious and righteous, glared at you out of a mass of curly hair.

Of course, what you didn't guess then was that Clarrie was jealous of *you*, of the way you could talk to anyone, ten to the dozen, and the fact that people saw you as the clever one.

Later, Granny would tell your mother, and you – meant to

look after Clarrie, not go picking quarrels – were in trouble all over again. And once more Clarrie said nothing, simply sat there looking at the floor, as your family reputation was being laid down: the selfish pesky one.

That was all before the war.

You think of Clarrie, too, in wartime: eighteen years old, statuesque and big-busted in her WAAF uniform, square shoulders held back the way she'd been trained, but still with a diffident set to her frame, and a tendency to giggle.

There's a scene that often comes back to you, although, for more than one reason, you wish that it didn't.

You were outside the Mess up at the camp: you, Clarrie and Clarrie's new boyfriend Robert, whom later she'd marry, a tall airman with glasses and prominent teeth and large ears.

You were nervous. He was a strait-laced chap, Robert, and you sensed he didn't like you. You knew in your heart by this time that Clarrie was jealous, of your small slim figure, your sense of fashion, the easy way you had of making friends, your academic success. You knew she felt it unfair, and of course Robert would know how she felt.

And something else was making you on edge: your own fiancé Jimmy. You were all going to the pictures, the four of you together, but you were being delayed because Jimmy was still in the Mess.

So handsome he was, Jimmy: hooded eyes and sharp jawline, and that wicked crooked grin, and everyone loved him for his charm. He was making you late, though, and Robert was obviously annoyed.

Clarrie gave her awkward little giggle, and you did what you always did when you were nervous, you gabbled. On and on you gabbled, you could hear yourself doing it. And then you saw it: Robert and Clarrie exchanging the look that told you what you'd done: cemented your reputation as the one who would never shut up or leave anyone alone.

*

'Olive?'

Always at the sound of her voice it's those images that first come to you.

She was ringing to tell you the details of Robert's funeral.

Her voice, as always, was plaintive – all those years of being bossed around by Robert – and today it was weak with grief.

You knew what she'd been going through, you'd gone through it yourself with Jimmy ten years before: trailing to the hospital every day, Robert so far gone that in the end he didn't know her, Clarrie hoping against hope, but knowing really she was watching him die.

This was Thursday, and the funeral, she said, would be Tuesday. 'Eleven o'clock.'

You were surprised it was so early. You repeated it: 'Eleven o'clock?' It was such a long way, down there in the South-West, and you up here in the Midlands. You'd have to go the previous day.

She said awkwardly: 'I'm afraid we wouldn't be able to put you up.'

You were a little hurt, and then quickly ashamed. Of course, Clarrie would have a houseful already – her three children and maybe their spouses, and even perhaps the grandchildren.

You said hastily, 'Oh, of course not!'

But you didn't much fancy staying in a hotel. You said, 'No problem, Clarrie, I'll come and get back in one day. I'll get a very early train.'

She didn't answer straight away. You were standing at the window and the silence went on so long you watched a wren pop out of the ivy on the wall outside and hop several steps up the greenery before popping back in again.

Then Clarrie said: 'Well, I'll give you instructions for getting to the crematorium.'

You were taken aback. Surely she'd want you to travel with her to the crematorium, the way she and Robert did with you when Jimmy died?

She was saying she had to go, and before you knew it she'd got off the phone.

You considered. Of course: the funeral was so early she reckoned you wouldn't have time to get to the house beforehand. Obviously, when you thought about it, you wouldn't. You chided yourself for letting those old childhood feelings of exclusion dog you into old age.

Elsie, too, your brother's widow, lived a distance from Clarrie, if not as far as you.

When Elsie rang you later that day, you said, 'I'm surprised they made it so early when we've got to travel.'

You thought of Elsie, as you first knew her, a skinny watchful girl who'd moved to the village from the town. A puny town girl you and Clarrie thought her, but then later your brother married her and she put you to shame, trudging in her wellies to help with the lambing, wading up to her neck with the trawlnet in the rock pools, gutting the fish in the back of the van.

And later, because Clarrie and Robert lived nearer than you and Jimmy, and so were able to visit more often, she and your brother and Clarrie and Robert became good friends.

Elsie said with surprise: 'Well, they couldn't have held it *much* later. It's at four in the afternoon.'

You told her, 'No, it's at eleven!'

How could Elsie have got it so wrong?

She said in bewilderment: 'I'll ring Clarrie back and check.'

Half an hour later she rang you again.

'Yes, Olive, the funeral's definitely at four.'

Was it you who had got it wrong?

She sounded strangely embarrassed.

But, no, you remembered, you'd repeated it to Clarrie: *Eleven o' clock?* with emphasis, precisely because you were so surprised, and she didn't contradict you.

'What did Clarrie say,' you asked Elsie, 'when you said I thought it was at eleven?'

There was a brief silence, and then Elsie said in a tight voice: 'I didn't mention it.'

This was even odder. You felt confused. Surely she'd have mentioned it, it was her reason for ringing Clarrie back and checking…

It hit you: Clarrie had lied to you about the time, and Elsie knew it.

Elsie said, with an air of quickly changing the subject, 'I'd rather get back the same night, but they're trying to persuade me to stay. They say they've got room.'

You reeled it back in your head, the conversation with Clarrie, and you heard it all now: the hesitancy, which you'd taken as the hesitancy of grief, with which she'd told you the time. The embarrassment: embarrassment at lying. And when she said she couldn't put you up, the stubborn note of old.

Then the silence when you said you'd come anyway: the silence of shock, and the old resentment at your persistence.

And if you were intent on coming anyway, she would give you instructions for getting to the crematorium. In other words, she wouldn't have you at the house.

But why?

'Why on earth would she do that?' your children cried. 'She isn't like that, Clarrie!'

Well, no, she wasn't. Were you wrong? Had you only imagined that Clarrie had said eleven o'clock? Had you imagined that you'd repeated it? Were you going senile? You could see that the thought had entered your middle-aged children's heads…

No, she wasn't like that, Clarrie, passive Clarrie who'd never say boo to a goose, who'd spent her life being bossed by others, who couldn't even make a phone call to you, her sister, without her husband Robert butting in on the extension.

And then it came to you. The quality of sound whenever Robert did that, picked up and listened in: slightly hollow, with a faint high background buzz. That sound was there again during the recent conversation.

Someone else had been listening in.

Someone else had heard you repeat, *Eleven o'clock?* and failed to contradict, failed to own up even to being there. Someone who didn't want you at the funeral.

Clarrie's eldest daughter Janet.

So often when you think of Janet, you see a chubby five-year-old in shorts with her hair in bunches, fishing in the shallow rock pools, those days after the war when you and Clarrie were still living in the village, when Robert was in Malaysia, and Clarrie, still wearing her green swimsuit, still giggly, was missing him and sad.

But also you think of Janet as a rangy young woman, handsome with Robert's strong features, standing here in your kitchen in the Midlands, one bright summer evening during the eighties, when she and her husband had been on business in Scotland and were calling in for tea on their way back down south. Just before they got here something had gone badly wrong with their car, but the local garage was shut for the evening, so though nothing was said, it was taken for granted they'd be staying the night.

You and she were washing up when she asked you, pointed and careful: 'Aunty Olive, why do you go to Granma's every single month to clean her house?'

You froze.

Yes, you *were* doing that. Your widowed mother was failing. She had a bad heart; for the past eighteen months her eyesight had been going, and now she was finding it difficult to walk. But then, Janet was implying, why did *you* need to go and clean for her, when you lived so far off and had a business to run, and when your brother's wife Elsie, a full-time housewife living right across the road, was looking after her already?

Janet stood with a bunch of gleaming teaspoons, waiting for an answer.

And the answer, the reason, bubbled in your chest and

pressed against your throat, and stuck.

A year before you had gone on one of your six-monthly visits back home.

You opened the door of your mother's cottage and found her sitting beside a dead congealed fire. Every surface was covered in dust, the carpet was unswept, dirty dishes were piled in the sink. Her eyes were red and weeping, and her prescription, made out two weeks before, lay on the sideboard, her medicine uncollected.

You tidied up and made her as comfortable as you could, then marched across the road to Elsie's.

A ghost answered the door. Her face was white; she was thinner than ever.

It was all too much for her, she told you, the shopping and cooking and cleaning for your mother: it was making her ill. She spoke in a hollow whisper: she'd lost her voice.

'*You'll* have to do it,' she told you. 'You'll just have to come down more often.'

You could hardly abandon your business, but you did agree to go for a few days every month, to take over the care of your mother and catch up on the cleaning and get in supplies.

Elsie added, 'She's *your* mother, after all,' which, after all, was fair enough.

But then she was Clarrie's mother too – Clarrie who didn't work, and lived so much nearer and came often to stay with Elsie and your brother for days of walking and fishing. But it was very quickly clear that Elsie had shared the problem with no one else, not even Clarrie.

Your heart sinking, you guessed why. In that place at that time, a rural village in the eighties, people would be all too ready to criticise a woman for abandoning her traditional role. And Robert, strait-laced Robert, could be more censorious than anyone. She was afraid of what he'd think of her. After all, she would know what he thought of you.

Clearly, she hadn't told your mother. 'Elsie will do that!'

your mother told you irritably as you washed the windows and laundered her sheets. She didn't understand why your visits had all of a sudden become so frequent, and why you spent them doing housework. You knew that she thought you a busybody, and probably that as usual you were jealous, jealous of her closeness with Elsie, and you couldn't deny – hating yourself for conforming to the family expectations – that under the circumstances, you *were* a little jealous, and not a little hurt.

You couldn't tell her the truth about Elsie yourself, you didn't feel you could betray her, and anyway, with your reputation, you'd look petty and vengeful. It didn't matter, you decided, as long as your mother was cared for. You wouldn't let it upset you: you, a woman running a business, with a life of her own elsewhere. You were bigger than that.

One day you went to collect your mother's pension and there in the post office was Clarrie's old friend Minnie. The girl with a mass of curls was now a stout matron with cropped hair, but as she made her way purposefully across towards you, the same old accusing look was her eyes. 'Olive,' she demanded, 'why do you keep coming down and making such a fuss of looking after your mother? You know there's no need. It's not fair on Elsie: it makes it look as if she's not bothering.'

You opened your mouth, but your unspoken pact with Elsie stopped any words.

She said, 'Well, Olive, we all know what you're like,' and turned away and walked out.

And now here it was happening with Janet your niece all over again, and once more, the truth, Elsie's secret, jammed in your throat.

Janet gave a nod. She placed the spoons on the table and, avoiding your eye, said with a knowing censorious smile: 'Well, we all know why you do it, Aunty Olive.'

What on earth could she be implying?

You knew they'd always seen you as selfish, but surely they couldn't think that you, a woman who owned a business, were after whatever your mother – whose house was rented, whose savings were probably non-existent – would leave when she died?

You were so upset you couldn't speak. You walked out of the kitchen and pretended to be busy in the utility room.

You thought of them all discussing you: Robert going on about you, the whole thing leaking out to be the talk of the village, Elsie keeping quiet, shamefully maybe, but secure in the protection of your reputation.

Just then the men came in from a stroll in the garden and your mouth jerked open, and before you could help it these words burst through the block in your throat: 'Well, Janet and Derek will have to get going: they'll need to drive slowly in that car.'

All three of them stared at you, disbelieving: surely Janet and Derek couldn't drive in that car, surely they were staying?

But then Jimmy gave you his Look.

Quizzical, shrewd it was, that look of Jimmy's. Very brief, sussing things out in a second or two, and then gone. The look of the conman, of course, a man who dealt in silk stockings during the war. But also the look of a man who *understands*, who knows exactly the score without a word being spoken. He didn't question you, or argue, he simply agreed.

And Janet and her husband had to leave, drive two hundred miles in a car that could conk out at any time, though thankfully it didn't.

You worried about them all evening, and were hugely relieved to hear next day that they'd got back safely after all. You worried they'd all be offended and furious, and expected a harangue from Robert. But neither he nor Clarrie mentioned what had happened, and you thought then that maybe Janet and Derek hadn't found it such a big deal, and you needn't have worried after all. You even thought that perhaps your notion of what they thought of you had all along been paranoid.

Now, at Robert's death, you understood it had been a huge deal. Why should they put Olive up, Janet would be thinking as she organised the funeral, when she did that to me? Why, come to that, should Olive even *be* at Dad's funeral, when he so disliked her? And Clarrie, so easily bullied, would be told what to say, while Janet listened in…

You ran it again in your mind, the conversation with Clarrie, and what you heard now was how miserable she sounded about it all.

So you didn't go to Robert's funeral. You sent flowers. They'd said they didn't want them, but you sent them specifically for Clarrie, to arrive when it was over, to express your solidarity as well as your condolence, to acknowledge that the problem was not between you and her.

And that day you tried to keep busy and think of other things. You washed some jumpers, and as you stood at the sink you kept seeing the wren take insects in its beak into the ivy where it must be nesting. Funny, the way it moved along in a straight smooth line, as if it didn't have legs, as if it were a mechanical thing on wheels, then flicked up and flew straight in, and the place where it had gone into the ivy was covered completely, so you'd never guess there was an entrance there.

In the evening Clarrie rang you to thank you for the flowers. She seemed more relaxed, and you felt relieved.

She told you in detail about the funeral, the number of cars they'd had to hire, the hotel they'd had to book to accommodate all of Richard's old colleagues, and the food they'd had for the reception. On and on she went, and that old feeling crept up on you: you began to have the sense that she was talking to herself, not you. She made no mention of your absence. There was, you began to realise, no hint of regret that you hadn't been there. By not going, you thought, you had let her off the hook and she was simply relieved.

You felt stung.

Elsie hadn't stayed over after all, and Clarrie said suddenly, as if it were a matter of great importance: 'I've rung Elsie, and she got home safely.'

At that – that discrimination – you couldn't help it, a bubble erupted from your throat: 'Clarrie, *why* wasn't I welcome at the funeral?'

It floated off and it couldn't be retrieved. There was a terrible silence, and you could picture her, shocked, confused, routed, shamed.

She said faintly, 'Of course you'd have been welcome!'

You could sense her horror, and were aghast yourself, but you were bursting with injustice, the way they'd always damned you as a gabbling pest while ensuring your silence and compliance. You were furious with Clarrie for always going along with it all, and with yourself for a lifetime of going along with it too.

You said, 'But Clarrie, you told me the funeral was at eleven when it was at four!'

She said, 'I didn't!' but it came out in a gasp.

You couldn't stop yourself. 'Well, you didn't invite me to the house. You said you'd tell me how to go straight to the crematorium.'

'I didn't!' She was starting to cry.

Then voices started up in the background. 'Mum, come away from the phone!' 'Don't talk to her!'

She said, her voice mushy with tears, 'Olive, I can't talk to you when you're like this,' and she put the phone down.

You stood there, still holding the receiver, a woman who was so self-centred she'd pick a quarrel with her sister on the day of her sister's husband's funeral.

And her children told her not to have anything to do with you again.

*

You know they did because she told you. She defied them.

That's the thing about Clarrie: she's often easily bullied, but she can also be stubborn.

She said, 'I want to sort out what happened between us.' Her voice was still plaintive, but there was an edge of determination. You had an image of her striding back out of the sea in her green swimsuit, water streaming from her strong limbs.

You said, 'Clarrie, it's best if we forget it.'

She sounded surprised. She said, upset and worried, 'But Olive, we're sisters, we can't have things unspoken between us.'

Funny, Clarrie being the one to plead, and you the one to insist on silence.

But after all, when it came to it, you couldn't have it all untangled it all with words; you couldn't have things dragged up. To explain why you sent Janet packing that evening would be to expose Elsie's deceit. And in order to stop Clarrie thinking you were being petty, you wouldn't resist explaining how they'd always all got you wrong, and – because it's still so painful – you'd go and mention that evening long ago outside the Mess, when Robert stared at you gabbling and made up his mind you were a bothersome pest. You'd have to say the real reason you were gabbling and panicking, and give away Jimmy's secret, which like Elsie's you've kept to this day.

So handsome he was, Jimmy, so charming, so popular with all the other airmen; everyone was drawn to him.

Looking back, in some deep part of you you'd half-guessed what he was up to as you waited, not just some black-market deal. You suppose if you hadn't you wouldn't have seen what you did that evening.

You were watching the Mess doorway over Robert's shoulder.

Someone came out, not Jimmy. He stopped to light a fag and stood there inhaling.

And then Jimmy did come out and you saw it, the look that passed between them: brief, gone in an instant, but a look of understanding, the score agreed without a word spoken. And then the other man looked away, and Jimmy passed him by and they were electric, you could see, with the effort of not acknowledging each other.

You'd half-guessed, but you didn't want to know.

For the whole of your marriage you didn't want to know.

Some things there's just no point dwelling on.

'Leave it, Clarrie,' you told her on the phone, and she did.

You put down the phone and listened to the wren's bub-bling eruptions of sound. Such a very little bird, and such a huge song.

Fresh Water

Charles Wilkinson

Whatever the boy was holding was a little too pale, and perhaps a little too pink, the Headmaster now realised, to have been extracted from a living body, but there was nevertheless something *arterial* about it that reminded him of the aftermath of open-heart surgery. And why on earth was Tanfield, normally one of his more tractable pupils, standing outside the front entrance of the school accompanied by a bemused, middle-aged woman whom the Headmaster had never seen before.

A few minutes earlier the Headmaster had been sitting securely in front of the computer in his study working on a new line management policy. It was one of the hottest days of a particularly hot summer, and the blinds were drawn. The lake was at its lowest level for many years and now so shallow that even the junior boys were being allowed to take the boat out unsupervised. In a glassy haze, a desultory cricket match was taking place on the main field, but the majority of the school had decamped to the swimming pool, and a distant splashing provided a soothing soundtrack to his administrative meditations. When the bell rang the Headmaster waited for the clatter of high heels on parquet flooring before recalling that he had given his secretary the day off. In many ways, it was, he thought, greatly to be regretted that it had become necessary to lock the front door during the day, but a series of thefts and acts of petty vandalism, not the least of which had been the disappearance of his wife's handbag from the hall, had resulted in a review of the school's security arrangements; and the dismal fact was that he was now sometimes obliged to answer the door himself. Although the school was located in a patch of countryside, London and its Home Counties outriders were now well over the horizon, colonizing the spaces between once isolated villages, tearing down the big old houses and building fifteen properties where one had stood before. Transport links had improved and on the main road outside the school gates the traffic was grid- locked by three in the afternoon. When the wind was in the right direction, you could just hear the trains carrying commuters to and from Kings Cross.

Dreading another incident, the Headmaster got up with a sigh and made his way to the door. The previous Saturday evening, whilt the school was in the Assembly Hall listening to the Summer Concert, one of the highlights of a crammed calendar of events, a gang of youths on bicycles had swept down the main drive, breaking the windows of parental cars parked on the verge, before escaping with a collection of mobile phones that police were still attempting to trace. As he opened the door, apprehension was rapidly followed by bewilderment, that was in turn succeeded by something like the beginning of process that would lead to an understanding of the significance of the extraordinary tableau before him: the unknown woman, whose expression seemed to echo his own perplexity; his pupil, Tanfield, paler and larger eyed than usual, cradling the third member of the trinity, as if it were all that remained of a once much-loved infant: a little flayed torso, a dull blue-pink heart, a tangle of veins and ribs like tiny claws. But the fact that Tanfield was dressed in the cross-country running team strip, now a dirty medicinal white, suggested that whatever bizarre concatenation of events had culminated in the scene before him could not be unconnected with Mr Vengelo, who, some thirty- five minutes previously, was to be seen running down a narrow gravel track enclosed by tall hedges that led to a wooden bridge. A hundred yards behind him, the first of his pursers, a tall boy with lank blond hair whose sun-reddened skin clashed with an orange and maroon t-shirt that had been bought at Camden Town market, clambered over the five-barred gate at the top of the hill. In the early '80s, when Mr Angus Vengelo had first joined the school it would not have been unusual to see him at the head of the field, or at least keeping comfortably abreast of some of the more athletic boys, but at the age of forty-nine his longstanding habit of drinking three pints of Benskins Best Bitter every night after work, combined with a penchant foa late night single malts, had finally undermined whatever claims to athleticism he might once have had. During his eighteen years as master in charge of the cross-country team, Vengelo had come to know every road, lane, path, hill, style, bridge, gate and stream within running distance of the school, and so when his fitness had first started to fade, it had been a simple matter to send the boys on a long route whilt he took a short cut that enabled him to emerge, much to their chagrin, triumphantly in front of them. Since the arrival of the new headmaster, whose fertile awareness of health and safety issues proliferated in the form of a multitude of memos, emails, notices, and letters to parents and colleagues, Vengelo had thought it prudent to stick to the same course as the boys, even though he had been reduced to the humiliating expedient of awarding himself a start of five to ten minutes. When even this ruse failed to keep him ahead of the pack for long, he had instructed them to wait at certain agreed points on the course: the bridge over the river Ver, the stile at the entrance to the park, the old oak tree, the entrance to the neo-Gothic pile, once the home of an American banker now a training college for teachers. Every year he got a little slower and arrived at the meeting points to increasingly ironic applause. But for once lassitude had infected even the keenest runners, and Mr Vengelo was able to enjoy the rare sensation of being in the lead, although strictly speaking the summer training sessions were not competitive.

As the ground dipped slightly, the weight of Mr Vengelo's stomach impelled him forward, giving him the pleasant sensation of having accelerated effortlessly. A decade ago he had been stones lighter; now although his legs and arms were still slim, his great belly, encased in a white, skin-tight top, peered over the rim of his black tracksuit bottom like a boiled egg jammed into a cup that was too small for it. In deference to the hot weather, and partly as a belated acknowledgement that the side parting was irrevocably out of fashion, Mr Vengelo, who already had a small head, had instructed his barber to cut his unruly, yolk-yellow hair close to his scalp, so that now, only faintly conscious of the absurdity of his appearance, as he half rolled, half ran down the hill, he appeared to be all stomach. Once he had reached the bottom of the hill, and the first bridge was in sight, Mr Vengelo gave himself an approbatory pat on his right thigh and smiled, a smile that soon dissolved in a pink pool of dismay as he realized that he had once again forgotten the mobile phone that he was supposed to take whenever he went running with the boys outside the school grounds. Then he remembered what had distracted him, he been on his way to get changed when he had met his colleague, the Head of English, John Craft, perhaps Vengelo's only ally in the Staff Common Room and the longest serving member of staff, who was making his way with a martyred expression to a session of the Curriculum Development Committee, one of the most influential of the many committees that had replaced traditional staff meetings.

'It's virtually impossible to sit down in this place. There isn't even time for a cup of coffee.'

'Would you rather go running with the boys?'

'I think I'm a bit old for that.'

'I think I'm a bit old for it too!'

At the moment that Vengelo met his cross-country group, which had been augmented by two Hong Kong Chinese, under the wellingtonia on the front lawn, John Craft arrived five minutes late for the Curriculum Development meeting. The Headmaster looked up from the document he was reading, but did not acknowledge him. Possibly in order to prevent people from getting up to make cups of coffee, the session, the fifth in under a fortnight, was taking place not in the comparative comfort of the staff room, but in the newest classroom block, a building that was principally noted for its tall glass windows, which could only be opened very slightly and with great difficulty, apparently a clever, post-modernist nod to Hardwick Hall. Everyone had taken off their jackets, and the Head of Science had even removed his tie.

When Craft sat down in the empty chair next him, his colleague leant over and whispered something about 'conical-shaped line management structures.' Resisting the temptation to point out that 'conical-shaped' was tautological, Craft made an attempt to understand what the headmaster was saying. Apparently it had once been thought that line management structures should be linear, subsequently a case had been made for a triangular model, but now the most advanced educational theorists favoured 'the conical-shaped option.'

At some point in the year Craft had been told who his line manager was. Since the arrival of the new headmaster, most of the colleagues with whom he had worked for years had been replaced by vigorous young South African or Australians, broad-shouldered games players with well-laundered hair, small moustaches and a freshly acquired determination to deliver their host country's National Curriculum; they were soon awarded 'positions of responsibility'. No doubt one of them was his 'line manager', whatever that meant. But which one? Craft pretended to make notes on a sheet of A4 paper. He had only three more years to go before retirement. There had been a time when he had contributed freely, perhaps even volubly, to staff discussions, but under the new dispensation his views had been poorly received. The thing to do, he had decided, was say as little as possible and try to avoid annoying anyone who might be important.

'Yes, but we must allocate at least one period a week for it. It's one of the main criteria for entry that schools in our locality are looking at. It's only right that all of our pupils should have opportunity to practise these vital skills.'

The Director of Studies was talking about next year's timetable, one of the few topics of genuine importance and interest. Craft put down his pencil.

'How are we going to fit these extra lessons in? The school day is quite long enough as it is, Todd.'

'No one is suggesting that the school day should be any longer. As I have made clear these lessons are already in place in the Junior School. What I am proposing is that the number of Classics periods should be reduced from three to two. I have discussed this with the Headmaster.'

'You have my support on this one, Todd.'

With dismay, Craft realised that they were proposing yet another reduction in the number of Latin lessons. Vengelo was the Head and only member of what was still called the Department of Classics, though Greek had been abandoned long ago. In spite of himself, Craft suddenly found that he was talking.

'Do you really think that Angus is going to be able to get them through their exams on two periods a week? I know for a fact that he's finding it hard enough on three.' They were looking at him. He had made the error of mentioning someone who was not present by name, a procedural legerdemain of the very worst sort. Discussion was supposed to take place at a suitably elevated level of abstraction, and proper nouns were seldom permitted to denote people unless the intention was unimpeachably phatic. Stung, he decided to continue.

'Anyway, I thought that the whole point of these verbal and non-verbal reasoning tests is that you can't cram for them. They're supposed to give some sort of objective assessment, aren't't they?'

The Headmaster was looking at him with an expression of impatience mingled with disgust.

'We would not be suggesting this change if there wasn't sound educational justification for it. Educational research has shown that children can and do improve their scores significantly. As for the Department of Classics, I'm sure they'll cope... John.'

With a sour shrug of the shoulders, Craft fell silent. In spite of his years of not disloyal service, his position at the school was less strong than he would have liked. One by one, the forms that he taught had ceased to understand a word that he was saying. At first incomprehension had been confined to the less able sets, but now even the scholarship streams were restless and apparently incapable of following stories and poems that had enthralled previous generations. At first, he had been able to buy a little time by jettisoning any text that had pretensions to literary merit, but now he was having difficulty finding a single book that was bad enough to command their attention. There was one form that couldn't't even watch a video in silence.

The Headmaster had begun to explain how form masters would assume responsibility for marking the weekly verbal reasoning tests and giving the results to the Director of Studies. It was hard to believe, Craft reflected, that the whole business would not end in Vengelo's enforced resignation. Although they were not especially close, they had worked together for almost two decades and had recently taken to meeting for a drink once a week, a shared revulsion to the new regime having at last created a bond. Craft wondered what he should say to his friend, who was at that moment running across the floodplains in the direction of the river Ver. In bad winters the field had been so wet as to have been impassable, were it not for the narrow causeway that connectedt the two bridges. But now the stream that had once flowed under the first bridge had disappeared and the Ver itself had been reduced to a sluggish green trickle. Nevertheless, there was something almost Japanese about the scene: the two bridges, the ancient trees, the delicate summer grasses. Vengelo stopped and turned round. The blond boy was now crossing the first bridge, but there was no sign of the others. He hoped that the Hong Kong Chinese were not lost. As he waited, he looked around and saw that a burnt-out car had been left close to the riverbank; he could just see that it had no number plates. It had probably been stolen in London, driven down here and doused in petrol. Giving way to a desire, which he recognised as rather childish, to be the first one to reach the bridge, Vengelo broke into a dignified trot. On the other side of the Ver was a park with mature trees and a grey Elizabethan house. Cattle sheltered under horse chestnuts. As he approached the riverbank, three anglers stood up. The tallest, a youth of about seventeen, wore a purple shell suit and a baseball cap. With him were a middle-aged woman in a tracksuit and a lilac top and a boy with gooseberry hair.

'Have you got a knife?'

The woman was speaking, and Vengelo noticed that she had hardly any teeth.

'Not on me.'

'It's just that we've caught this lobster.'

'A lobster?'

Vengelo was assailed by a sudden sybaritic vision: what else were they going to fish out of the river: a bottle of champagne in an ice bucket, a crisp salad and dish of buttered new potatoes?

'Yes, we've caught this lobster.'

'Congratulations!'

'No, you don't understand. We don't want it. We want to put it back, but we can't; it's stuck on the line.'

The pale blue - pink creature, which was probably some species of freshwater crayfish, lay still on grass; the barb at the end of line was stuck deep into its side.

'I'm sorry, I can't help you.'

As the runners arrived, they too began to look at the crayfish, and the tall youth, who had the appearance of being slightly simple, questioned them in the hope that they would somehow be able to liberate the creature. Tanfield, the only boy to be correctly dressed in the official cross-country strip, had knelt down and was examining the barb carefully. Irritated, Vengelo ordered the runners to the other side of the bridge.

Once they were in the park the questions came:

'Can't we go swimming?'

'Not today.'

'Why not?'

'The river's too shallow.'

'Aren't you going to rescue those people's lobster?'

'It's not a lobster.'

'Please let us go swimming, sir; it's hot, sir.'

'Oh all right. You can splash about, but you mustn't swim. It's not deep enough. Has anyone seen Wu and Shu?'

No one had seen Wu and Shu. Perhaps they'd been left so far behind that they'd decided to make their own back to school. If anyone from the senior management team saw them return unaccompanied …

'It's Tanfield, sir. He's been wounded, sir. You must come at once.'

Vengelo had been dimly aware of commotion on the other side of the river. He hurriedly crossed the bridge to find an apologetic Tanfield holding the crayfish and the line of the fishing root. It appeared that Tanfield, driven by misguided compassion and curiosity, had remained with the angler who had then persuaded him to free the creature; in doing so, he had somehow ended up with a barb in his forefinger. The only consolation was that Tanfield had remained calm and there was surprisingly little blood.

'Go on, sir. I don't mind if you just rip it out.'

Vengelo inspected the finger a little more closely and then gave an experimental tug. There was no gentle way of easing the barb out. It would just have to stay where it was.

'Can we have our rod back?'

'Be quiet. I'm thinking.'

'You can't leave with our rod.   '

'You'll just have to chew through the line won't you.'

Just how many of the school's health and safety regulations had he broken? He'd forgotten the mobile phone, omitted to fill in a risk assessment form, lost two members of his group and now the son of one of the most influential parents had been wounded in an encounter with some sort of lobster. At seven o'clock he was due to meet John Craft in the Cat and Fiddle. It was the one occasion of the week when he had company, the one time when he had an opportunity to exercise a little dry Scottish humour, and he had been looking forward to telling him about his meeting with Murray Donoghue, the newly appointed Australian Deputy Headmaster, who had been in charge of break detention when Mr Vengelo had been to see him that morning. Two boys in the front row looked up and smirked.

'And what can I do for you, Mr Vengelo?'

A parody of the British manner. General laughter and the sound of a pencil case falling to floor. Donoghue raised a hand for silence before turning to Mr Vengelo, who was craning confidentially towards him. It would be something to do with the running club. Not so much a disaster waiting happen as one parading itself before their very eyes, that's what he'd told the Headmaster.

'It's about my club. In this very hot weather, I've been letting the boys have a dip in the Ver. They've always been allowed to do this, but I thought I better just check that this is still O.K.'

Donoghue looked at Mr Vengelo closely. With that belly on him and in this heat it would be a miracle if he made it round. The guy should appoint a spade monitor and tell the kids to bury him where he falls. And what was the paratrooper's haircut about?

'Well, strictly speaking you should have a qualified swimming pool warden present. Are you sure you want to go running in this heat?'

'They're looking forward to it. It's more of a fun run than a training session. The Ver's not very deep at the moment. Frankly, it would be an achievement to drown.'

Something of the freedom of his childhood on a Queensland farm came back to him. The kids were twelve to thirteen years old, for Christ's sake. Why couldn't they paddle in a stream that came up to their ankles?

'Well O.K. - but I didn't say so.'

'Sorry to bother you, but there are just so many…'

'You don't have to tell me. Remember to fill in a risk assessment form.'

As the door closed behind Veneglo, Donoghue sighed. Strictly speaking it would have been better to put a stop to the whole thing, but with the curriculum development committee meeting in games time they were short staffed. And it was hard to know how to treat these old guys, Vengelo and the other one, the one with the white face who looked as if he was actually dying, John Craft, who three hours later, shifted restlessly in one of the most ergonomically unsatisfactory chairs ever to have been designed, whilt two and a half miles away from the room in which the Curriculum Development Committee was meeting, the tall youth in the purple shell suit succeeded in biting through the line, thus releasing Tanfield and regaining control of the rod, at the very moment that the Headmaster began a ten minute speech on the ways in which he saw curriculum development developing, which concluded as Tanfield and Mr Vengelo ran-walked up the gravel drive towards the neo-Gothic mansion that had once housed a teacher training college, and where a secretary, who was just about to leave for the day, was persuaded to drive Tanfield, still holding the creature, back to school, leaving Mr Vengelo, alone on the drive and not within supervisory distance of any of his pupils, to consider the repercussions of entrusting a pupil in his care to an adult whom he had never seen before, a lady now alone with a strange child, who was holding what appeared to be a crayfish resting on a bed of spaghetti, as he gave directions to the school, where the Headmaster had left the new classroom block and was walking back into his cool dark study, whilst Mr Vengelo waited for the cross-country runners to join him and wondered what on earth had happened to Wu and Shu, who had clearly made no attempt to keep up with the others and would have to report to the study, in which the Headmaster would soon be seated in front of his computer, with just five minutes to work on his revisions to his policy document on line management, before a red car would come down the long drive from the main road and two figures, a middle-aged woman and a boy carrying a crayfish/ small fresh water lobster, would get out and walk towards the front door which is once again locked, for it seven o'clock and most of the staff and pupils have gone home. It is a little cooler and the evening light is a deeper shade of sherry-gold. A few boarders with brightly striped towels over their shoulders wander past the rose garden on their way to the swimming pool, from which a faint splashing can still be heard. An angora rabbit has escaped from the animal hutch and sits on the cricket pitch. In a bungalow at the edge of Barnet the secretary thinks about the school whose sign she has driven past for fifteen years, but whose buildings she had never seen until today; she thinks of the long drive, the boys playing croquet on the front lawn, so small beneath the ancient trees; the wisteria hanging over the porch, the sun-polished ivy. She could never have afforded a place like that for her son. Bandaged, Tanfield has returned from Accident and Emergency and is using his one good hand to access the Internet. Soon he will find his creature, the one that he rescued and put in the lake. He cannot believe that it might already have been dead. He learns that crayfish can be called yabbies, ghost shrimps, crawdads, mudbugs, carmels, spoondogs and tiny creek lobsters. The study of crayfish is astacology, and they like crevices. Some are good at escaping and others, to judge from the pictures, are best served with a side salad. A few are kept as pets. He hopes his crayfish will be happy in its new home. John Craft reminds his wife that he is going to the pub and takes the car keys off the hall table. It isn't going to be a good evening. Somehow he must find a tactful way to warn Vengelo. Mind you, at this rate it looks as if they will both be for the chop. He still cannot forget the way that his colleagues were looking at him, as if he were some sort of antiquated ghost, perhaps the one with a face like 'crumpled linen' in... was it M. R. James? An author he'd long ago had to stop reading to the children. Since it is the one evening when he knows he will have company, Mr Vengelo has left his edition of Horace in his bedroom. It has been a difficult day, but he is a little more cheerful now. The Tanfields were surprisingly understanding, and apparently Accident and Emergency had been extraordinarily efficient. A relief to learn that he had done the right thing in leaving the barb exactly where it was. He represses a shudder when he remembers how close he came to pulling it out. Once inside the Cat and Fiddle he is surprised to find it half empty. No doubt most of the customers are in the beer garden. He is looking forward to telling Craft about Murray Dohoghue and the risk assessment form. What these people are incapable of understanding is that the real dangers are often unforeseeable. How could he possibly have anticipated the incident with the lobster or whatever it was? Perhaps they would now ask him to write a policy document: 'Crustaces and Cross-Country Running.' The Polish barman wonders why the man with the funny haircut is laughing. In the study, which is coolest room in the school, the Headmaster has finished his document on line management. Now he has just one more task before he can go home. Vengelo has become impossible. Forcing a pupil into a complete stranger's car is utterly unacceptable and flies in the face of everything that the school's child protection policy has been set up to achieve. Of course having to get rid of a member of staff at this point in the academic year is far from ideal, but the examinations are over and if a suitable replacement cannot found for September it will not be a disaster if Classics is dropped altogether. Few schools seemed to want it. Of course, some parents would object, but they would be a tiny minority. As he lifts up the phone, he is sure the Chairman of the Governors will agree. At the bottom of the lake the crayfish lies next to the wheel of an old bicycle. Even if it is still alive, it will not survive for long. No, it is lost now, along with all those who can only dream of fresh water.

The End of the World

CS Mee

As the end of the world drew nearer, everyone began to think with pre-emptive nostalgia about all the things that would soon be gone. They gathered in living rooms across the country to reminisce over tea and biscuits. At first they were quiet, each in a corner, wrapped in their own private thoughts. Long moments would pass, the air warm and damp with thinking. Then, as if poked awake and roused from their reverie, they would turn to each other and begin to share their reflections.

'I was just remembering autumn leaves,' someone would say, 'how bright they were, aflame on the trees, how crunchy on the ground.'

'And I was thinking of Saturday afternoons,' another would add, 'so full of promise, so luxuriously long.'

Then a third would join in, 'and what about the peacocks: their jewelled plumes, their tiny brains, their beady eyes, their tasty meat.'

They mused over Nature with its paraphernalia of mountains and rivers, lakes and trees, birds and animals and mulch. They talked about taking walks in it, how they would collect bits of it to decorate the mantelpiece, how it would stick to their shoes and dirty the carpet. They remembered when it came creeping into the house through a hole in the skirting board and had to be dealt with.

For hours and days, people sat reminding each other of all things memorable and forgettable that would soon perish with the end of the world. Now that the initial panic was over they were happy to spend their time quietly reminiscing. Nobody recalled how talk of the end had first arisen, nobody could name the origin of that terrible news, but they were all certain that they would soon witness the end of everything. When the rumours had started everyone was filled with apocalyptic dread; mayhem had lurked, anarchy had loomed, and pandemonium had kept the children awake all night. Before long certainty had submersed doubt, assertion had beaten back denial, and acceptance now ruled over the land. Now, in the calm before the end of everything, the people wanted to remember it all before it was too late.

The conversation drifted onto pies and they discussed apple pies and apricot pies, blackberry pies and blueberry pies. They considered cottage, Cornish, banoffee, toffee, steak and kidney, damson, rhubarb crumble pies. They lingered over pork pies and pumpkin pies, pies with crusts and pies without, lidded pies and latticed pies, upside-down pies and right-way-up pies, and the very best of all: grandmothers' homemade pies.

Being nostalgic was taking such a long time that soon they realised the end of the world had drawn closer and nobody had even left the house yet. All the talk of pies had made them hungry and what they wanted now was a last taste of those pies that grandmothers made so well.

Across the land elderly women were roused from their rocking chairs, had their knitting needles and whittling knives confiscated, and were coaxed back into the kitchen. Adjusting their sight and rubbing sore hips, they found their bearings, located pastry cutters and scraped the blackened crust out of baking tins. Then they fired up ranges and were soon sticky to the elbows with flour and butter. Sweet odours wafted out into the streets and before long the whole country smelled of pastries and cakes, steamed puddings and jams. The nation salivated in anticipation.

When the oven gloves were off and warm golden pies lay ready to be sliced on crisp white doilies, the country fell silent. Then all that could be heard was the barely audible flaking of pastry, the crumbling of cakes, the seeping of jam, the oozing of cream and the licking of contented lips by contented tongues. Since it was the end of the world, everyone was allowed a second helping and an extra dollop of custard. Elevenses carried on into lunch and beyond and soon it was time for afternoon tea. A fresh cake lay waiting on a new doily, another pile of home-baked scones, another tart, another crumble. The nation's nostalgic taste buds were sated.

Now that the grandmothers had returned to the kitchen there was no holding them back; flour and sugar coated every surface like a light snowfall, the floor was sticky with slicks of treacle and the nation's cake-stands sank beneath the weight of their ever-mounting load. There was such a rush on tea that the shops ran out and national stocks were desperately low. Every cup of tea was drunk as though it might be the last, and well it might. Meanwhile, the people were gaining weight by the ounce, the pound, the stone. Sated taste buds soon began to tire, stomachs grumbled and sweet teeth turned sour. The extra slice, the fourth serving, the ice-cream scoop were all politely but firmly declined. The cakes and pies began to pile up uneaten, filling cupboards and kitchen surfaces, going stale in biscuit tins and under plastic wrap.

With the end of the world drawing nearer and the grandmothers baking relentlessly, everyone decided to visit their distant relatives and friends, to see them all one final time, to offload a fruitcake and a batch of shortbread.

Packing up their hampers, they got into their cars and all set off at once.

Roads and motorways were immediately jammed as everyone made their way to the houses of college friends, old work colleagues and first cousins twice removed. Bumper to bumper and backed up down the slip roads they crawled impatiently on. Journeys that usually lasted a couple of hours now took days and by the time everyone arrived they were all tired and hungry and grumpy. Up and down the land the weary travellers rang the doorbells of empty houses to no avail, since their occupants were away visiting relatives and friends.

Foul moods brewed.

Some chose to sit out in the garden and wait, others got back in their cars and returned home. Traffic jams and tempers ensued. Some of the returning drivers crossed paths with the very relatives and friends they had set out to see and, catching sight of each other across the central reservation, they stopped their cars in the middle of the motorway and rolled down their windows, ready for a good natter. Then cars were queuing and beeping for miles, waiting for the reunited drivers to pull off the road and carry on their chitchat in a service station. Others returned home to find distant relatives and long-lost friends crowded onto the front lawn.

The relief of reunion lightened the mood. Stale cakes were unwrapped, hardened scones handed out, teabags distributed. Now that most of the black tea was finished they had to make do with the less popular teas, the stranger fruit flavours and the homeopathic infusions. Others resorted to coffee.

The visitors settled in and they spent a long while catching up with each other. They were soon in full flow, dwelling on the good old days and reminiscing with more than an occasional tear, when a child crawled out from under the sofa and interrupted them.

'When will it be the end?' he asked.

'And, his sister added, from her perch on an armrest, 'how will it end?'

The adults paused in amazement, and turned to each other with questioning eyes. They had been so fixed on the past that they had forgotten about the imminent future, but now they left their memories behind and began to foretell what lay ahead.

'It will end with a catastrophic meteorite,' someone said, 'sending the Earth spinning off its axis, hurtling into the furthest coldest reaches of the universe.'

'Four horsemen will descend from the heavens,' another added, 'riding horses white and red and black and pale.'

Then a third joined in, 'and the dinosaurs will return, with their shredding claws, their gnashing teeth, their crushing feet, their piercing antlers.'

Each person took a turn speculating and at first all predictions were considered equally possible, equally frightening a prospect. Then friendly competition developed as people began to scoff at each other's ideas and dismiss the more esoteric suggestions. Soon rival groups formed, backing one catastrophe over another: alien invasions vied with the death of the sun, black holes competed with gamma ray bursts and the Big Crunch entered the race as an outside contender. Before long the conversations became heated and foul moods brewed once more. Revelations was cited emphatically, Nostradamus was consulted repeatedly, Ragnarök was evoked angrily and voices were raised over the end of the Mayan calendar. The grandmothers joined in from the kitchen, shouting out their predictions while they waited for the brownies to brown. Patience was tested, the air buzzed with tension; tempers frayed and began to unravel. Eventually old grievances surfaced, forgotten arguments were remembered and rows broke out as inheritances were disputed, infidelities alleged and vengeances sought. Teacups were overturned, plates were smashed, furniture was upended, brownie crumbs were ground into the carpet.

Anarchy loomed large.

Sensing that calamity was near, the government attempted to intervene. They broadcast soothing music over the radio, they distributed leaflets promoting inner peace, they pasted up posters with calming mantras, they even tried to tax bad tempers. In due course they sent out teams of psychologists, therapists and hostage negotiators to broker reconciliations.

The mediators began by chasing the grandmothers out of the kitchens, handing back their balls of twine and their chisels and returning them to their armchairs. The indigestion and heartburn abated.

Amit the shouting and the broken furniture the situation still looked dire, but then the weather took a nasty turn. Hailstones rattled at the windows, distracting everyone from their fighting and reminding them to get home and feed the parrots. Across the land arguments were hastily resolved and where differences were irreconcilable agreements to disagree were ratified. Hands were shaken. Backs were patted. Shoulders rubbed. There were occasional hugs. The visitors drove back home and settled down to watch the weather and wait for the meteorites. For days and weeks the sky was overcast and there was a persistent drizzle. A nasty gale whipped the roof off the shed and snow delayed the trains.

Meanwhile, the historians were having a miserable time. At first they had been excited about the end of the world because it would bring the end of History and they could put the last full stop on that great narrative. Although nobody knew exactly when the end would come, each was eager to be the first to declare History finished. They tried to pre-empt each other, announcing the end to steal the limelight. History thwarted them; each time they thought the final end had come something else happened. Some had already written THE END and crossed it out to add another paragraph several times and their books were becoming untidy. Others had run out of pages and had to paste in extra ones, then they ran out of glue and had to use tape, which was even messier. Soon the history books were bulging with extra pages but nobody would contemplate starting a new book so close to the end.

It was such a long time since the end of the world had begun that people were starting to get restless. The government debated whether they could bring proceedings forward, but they quickly fell to bickering and infighting and the nation resolved to await the real end.

They did not have to wait for long.

Rumours began to circulate that the end was imminent; excited murmuring swept the country like a Mexican wave. People gathered in preparation to witness the end, crowding on street corners, huddling in pubs, congregating in town squares. They stood on cliff tops and beaches, expecting the end to come from the sea. The weather had improved, so they brought picnics and tents and camped out to wait. Some had caviar and champagne, others had only stale muffins and dry brownies. One family even had a flask of hot tea, but they pretended it was coffee to avoid envy. Soon there were great crowds on the cliffs and beaches, arranged on deck chairs and blankets, staring out to sea as if they were watching a film. The government gave up their infighting and came out to join the nation, the grandmothers hobbled along and all the historians were there, ready with their pens poised to write their final THE END.

As day turned to dusk, silence fell upon the gathered nation and they watched the sun set for the last time. It was a grand finale, a glorious exit, with a sky of oranges and reds and purple-blues and strips of cloud like pink candy strewn out over the horizon. The sun sank into the sea, almost reluctantly, and darkness fell. Clouds gathered, the moon hid away and no star shone. It was cold and dark at the end of the world. As the night advanced it became unbearably chilly and everyone started grumbling that they would rather see out the end wrapped up warm in their beds. Nobody moved from the shore. Nobody left. They all knew that the end of the world was just about to begin.

It started a little before dawn. Out of the night a sinister light began to gather on the horizon. Grey fingers reached up into the sky, growing paler and bluer as doom began to unfold. Everyone was silent, all eyes on the horizon, all watching aghast. Something was coming for them, coming from beyond the sea, growing up into the sky, looming large over the water. They wondered if it was the many-tentacled Hydra lifting up out of the ocean to swallow them up, or the Cosmic Boa Constrictor swooping through space to encircle the Earth and wrap them in its crushing grip. They watched agog, each silently betting.

Then it came.

At first a band of flame appeared on the horizon, glowing red like the blood of demons. Then it began to rise slowly into the sky, growing ever brighter and ever greater. Soon the mere sight of it became unbearable, burning into their retina. They turned their eyes away in pain as the light formed into a giant ball of fire, ever rising, drawing ever nearer. Soon the evil radiance was so intense it dazzled the whole sky.

The people leapt to their feet in terror. Panic and mayhem broke out on the shore. Anarchy released its dark forces. Some tried to run back, to escape inland, while others scrambled forwards into the shallows, stretching out their arms to embrace their fate. In the confusion husbands lost wives, parents lost children, children lost teddy bears, teddy bears lost their noses. All were screaming and struggling on the beach, the sand was kicked into a melee like gritty custard.

The flaming sphere continued its inevitable path. Now they could feel its heat on their skin, ready to blister them into ashes, about to frazzle each one to vapour. Soon sparks would land ashore, setting the trees alight, hissing into the waves, heating the sea to a boil. There was more mayhem, with screaming and cursing and begging and shrieking and crying and praying and weeping and shouting. The fire grew ever closer and ever hotter. Anarchy held the nation in an ever-tighter clasp. The government collapsed, the historians lost their books in the shallows, the grandmothers abandoned their whittling.

After a while, with all the screaming and cursing and running around, everyone had become very tired and had a sore throat. They began to give up and sit down, awaiting impending doom. Anarchy slunk off, leaving weary calm to restore some order. Family members recovered family members; friends found friends and all sat down to take a rest. They kept watch on the scorching globe of fire that would soon bring the end of the world. It crept higher and higher, appearing to move away from the Earth. Now its heat had stabilised at a temperature that was almost pleasant. Now they knew that it would rise to the top of the sky and then drop like a firebomb to obliterate them all. They waited in calm and silence for the end. Someone handed round a packet of digestives. They nibbled their biscuits and eyed the fireball, waiting.

The end of the world drew ever nearer.

Unthologists

Elizabeth Baines' collection of short stories, *Balancing on the Edge of the World*, is published by Salt, who also published her two short novels, *Too Many Magpies* and *The Birth Machine*. She has also written prizewinning plays for radio and stage.

Roelof Bakker is the founder of Negative Press London. He is the editor of *Still: Short Stories Inspired by Photographs of Vacated Spaces* (Negative Press London, 2012), which was shortlisted in the Saboteur Awards 2013 for Best Mixed Anthology. *Strong Room*, a collaboration with artist Jane Wildgoose, was published January 2014. 'Red' is his first published story. www.rbakker.com, www.neg-press.com

Sarah Bower is a prize-winning short story writer and the author of two critically acclaimed historical novels, *The Needle in the Blood* (Susan Hill's Novel of the Year 2007) and *The Book of Love* (published in the US as *Sins of the House of Borgia*) Her work has been translated into nine languages. *Sins of the House of Borgia* was an international bestseller. Her third novel, *Erosion*, is scheduled for publication in 2013. She is currently working on a short story commission for BBC Radio 4. Sarah lives in Suffolk and is presently in residence at Lingnan University, Hong Kong.

Garrie Fletcher writes and performs in Birmingham. He has appeared on many occasions at City Voices, in Wolverhampton, Poetry Bites, in Birmingham and the launch night of Naked Lungs. His work has been published both online and in print including *The Canon's Mouth, The Birmingham Post* and *3am. Magazine*, he has the starting poem on the Polesworth Poetry Trail and has had poetry broadcast on Radio Wildfire. An early collection of his writing entitled *Notown* is available from www.blackheathbooks.org.uk and his poetry can also be found in the latest anthology from Offa's Press entitled *We're All In This Together*, the *Earth Love* anthology and the first issue of *Naked Lungs*.

Victoria Heath was born in Dublin, grew up in Lincolnshire and now lives in Brighton where she writes short stories and works as an editor. Her stories have been published by *Structo* and shortlisted for the 2012 Bridport Prize.

Maggie Ling has been a fashion designer and illustrator, children's charity worker, children's book illustrator, cartoonist and occasional poet, her work appearing in books, magazines and newspapers, a cartoon collection published by Virgin Books. Leaving London for the Suffolk coast, she began writing fiction. Since then poems have appeared in *Mslexia* and in *Lines in the Sand*: New Writing on War and Peace (Frances Lincoln 2004), short stories shortlisted by *Mslexia* and for the Asham Award, longlisted by Cinnamon Press and Fish Publishing, commended by Words and Women, and published in Unthology 1 (Unthank Books 2010) and the Asham Award-winning anthology *Something Was There* (Virago 2011).

Mark Mayes has published short stories and poems in literary magazines and anthologies including: *The Reader, Staple New Writing, The Interpreter's House, Other Poetry, The Waterlog* (Two Rivers Press), *True To Life* (Ruskin Anthology), *Fire*, and *The Shop*. In 2010 he was shortlisted for the Bridport Prize, and has had work broadcast on BBC Radio 4. He has recently completed his first novel, and a book-length story for children.

C. S. Mee grew up in Birkenhead and currently lives in Switzerland. She recently completed an MA in Creative Writing with Lancaster University. *The End of the World'* was her first short story and was a runner-up in the 2011 *Short Fiction* contest. Her fiction has since appeared in *Prole* and *Wasafiri* and is forthcoming in Salt's *New Writing* anthology. She won the Wasafiri New Writing Prize 2012 and came third in the Neil Gunn Writing Competition 2013. She is working on a novel.

Andrew Oldham is an international award winning writer and poet. His fiction has appeared in *Transmission, The Times Magazine* online and *Next Stop Hope*. Andrew was the runner up in the Dead Ink Flash Fiction Competition 2012 and is a past Jerwood-Arvon nominee. His poetry has been heard on BBC Radio Four's *Poetry Please* and has been read in *Ambit, The London Magazine* and *North American Review*. His first collection was *Ghosts of a Low Moon* (Lapwing, Belfast 2010) and in 2013 he narrated the short poetry film *Chalk Trace* (Blanche Pictures/Channel 4). He teaches Creative Writing and is a journalist for *The Guardian* blog.

Angela Readman completed her MA at The University of Northumbria. Her stories have been short listed in The Costa Short Story Prize, The Bristol Short Story Prize, The Asham Award and The Short Story Competition. She has been published in *Unthology* and in journals online including *Smokelong Quarterly, Metazen* and *Pank*. She is currently writing a collection.

John David Rutter writes short stories. He completed an MA at Lancaster University and is currently working on a short story PhD at Edge Hill University. His stories have been published in the *Lancashire Evening Post* and he was Guest Editor of Lancashire Writing Hub during 2012.

Jose Varghese is an English teacher from India, working at Jazan University, Saudi Arabia. His PhD is in Post-Colonial Fiction and he is currently working on a research project on the works of Hanif Kureishi. His collection of poems *Silver Painted Gandhi and Other Poems was* listed in Grace Cavalieri's Best Reading for Fall 2009, in *Montserrat Review*. His poems and stories have appeared in Indian and international journals/anthologies like *The Salt Anthology of New Writing 2013, The River Muse, Chandrabhaga, Kavya Bharati, Muse India, Poetry Chain, Postcolonial Text, Remarkings, Dusun* and *The Four Quarters Magazine*. He is the founder and chief editor of *Lakeview International Journal of Literature and Arts*.

Charles Wilkinson: born Birmingham 1950. Educated at the universities of Lancaster, East Anglia and Trinity College, Dublin. Publications: *The Snowman and Other Po*ems (Iron Press, 1978) and *The Pain Tree and Other Stories* (London Magazine Editions, 2000). His stories have appeared in *Best Short Stories 1990* (Heinemann), *Best English Short Stories* (Norton), *Midwinter Mysteries* (Little, Brown) and *Unthology 2* and *Unthology 3* (Unthank Books). His recent work has appeared in *Poetry Wales, Poetry Salzburg, Earthlines, Other Poetry, The Warwick Review, Tears in the Fence, Shearsman, The SHOp* and other literary magazines and anthologies. He lives in Presteigne, Powys.